XENO'S PARADOX

Borgo Press Fiction by BRIAN STABLEFORD

XENO'S PARADOX

A TALE OF THE BIOTECH REVOLUTION

BRIAN STABLEFORD

THE BORGO PRESS
MMXI

XENO'S PARADOX

FIRST EDITION

Published by Wildside Press LLC

www.wildsidebooks.com

DEDICATION

For Sally

CONTENTS

AUTHOR'S NOTE

ALTHOUGH THIS STORY is self-contained, it is a sequel to two earlier stories in the series to which it belongs. "Hidden Agendas" (in *The Tree of Life and Other Tales of the Biotech Revolution*, Borgo Press, 2007) introduced the character of Carly Maclaine and his clone parent, while "Snowball in Hell" (in *Designer Genes and Other Tales of the Biotech Revolution*, Five-Star, 2004) detailed the immediate outcome of the experiments in Applied Homeotics conduced by Dr. Hemans and his colleagues.

CHAPTER ONE

I HAD JUST FINISHED a two o'clock seminar on the application of
xenogenetic techniques to the enhancement of plant motility,
and I was feeling equally pleased with the typical eloquence that
my explanations had displayed and the expressions of admira-
tion that had shown in the faces of one or two of the female
undergraduates.

I knew, in my heart of hearts, that all was not well with the
world, but I was clinging to my contentment with the illusion
created by the cultural insulation cocooning the university,
preserving an impression of enduring calm and order. I probably had a certain euphoric bounce in my step as I left the room,
having ushered the students out in advance. The bounce lasted
all the way back of my lab, and I remember greeting the assistant who tended the seedlings in the outer lab with a cheerful
bonhomie that wasn't entirely typical of my personality.

I wove my way through the narrow and winding pathways
left in my inner sanctum by the careful arrangement of my
finest mature specimens to my desk in the far corner, where I
set my palm-prompter down and immediately turned in order
to bid an equally cheerful hello to the multitudinous host of my
most intimate companions. I had barely got through the first
syllable, though, when there was a knock on the door. My assistant had been well-trained in the arts of interception, and I knew
that he would not have let any random caller reach the door of
my minuscule empire, so I assumed that it must be Paula or
Marianne, dropping in to tell me that she loved me.

My good mood evaporated in a trice, however, when I saw the man who was standing in the outer lab, looking round curiously at all the immature Venus fly-traps, various *Mimosa* species and tall sheaves of porcupine-grass. Not unnaturally, it was the Venus fly-traps that were catching and holding his attention; being natural exhibitionists, they always trapped the gaze of unwary newcomers. Even when he redirected his eyes at my face, he only held them there for a fraction of a second before peering over my shoulders at the giants of the carnivorous species distributed around the room, amid the similarly giant Mimosas and the huge clumps of modified *Stirpa*.

He stepped forward as if to come in and take a closer look, but I blocked the doorway, mentally pulling up the drawbridge and lowering the portcullis. There was no way that someone like him was getting into my fortress without a fight.

"So this is where you've been hiding all these years," he observed, instead. It wasn't exactly a cannon-shot, but it was an assault of sorts, however mild his tone might be.

I hadn't been hiding, any more than he had been looking for me. I assumed that he hadn't even been doing any actual spying—not personally at any rate. He had had assistants to do that for him back in the day, and he had probably enjoyed some professional advancement since then. Social mobility had slowed down as human longevity had increased, but the inexorable expansion of the Commonwealth's governmental apparatus meant that opportunities were always opening up in its higher echelons.

It was almost twenty years since I'd last clapped eyes on him, and an awful lot of data had flowed through the conduits of the WorldWeb in the meantime, but he looked much the same, and I didn't suppose for a moment that the significance of his strictly-disciplined appearance had changed either. He repented of his careless remark, though. "Good afternoon, Mr. Maclaine," he said, starting again with carefully-manufactured politeness. "It's been a long time."

"Mr. Chesterton," I said, with a lack of enthusiasm that was utterly unfeigned. "Still working for PEST Control? As you must know perfectly well, it's *Doctor* Maclaine, at least within these walls."

The last time I had seen Alexander Chesterton, I had told him that we had nothing further to say to one another, then or ever—but he hadn't agreed with me at the time and might have been forgiven for wearing an "I told you so" expression now. In fact, he had much better self-control than that. He was doing his level best to look even more serious than was his wont, as if giving new meaning to the phrase "deadly earnest."

"The Department of Political and Environmental Security, Transfiguration and Control had been superseded before you were born, Dr. Maclaine," he said. "That was one of your name-sake's phrases. I had hoped that you might have moved on from all that, now that you've built a career of your own."

"I have moved on," I told him. "I don't have any involvement with the various kinds of work that Cade was involved with in his prime, or the various kinds of paranoia that he carried to his grave." For safety's sake, I added: "And I haven't had any contact whatsoever with Napoleon since he went on the run."

Unlike its predecessors, the last statement was a downright lie—but I felt entitled to a certain paranoia of my own, given that the direct descendants of PEST Control now seemed to consider rogue AIs to be the most significant chaotic flies in the ointment of World Order. You wouldn't have known it from watching the news, of course, but I had an inside source. I knew the arcane code-names of the individuals who had no photographs to pin up on the walls of Secret Police HQ—Xeno, Ulysses, Oberon and Napoleon were those at the head of the list—and I knew that the euphemistically-named Ministry of Information was becoming very worried indeed about the possibility that open hostilities might break out at any moment, the outcome of which would be far from certain. Given that the Repopulation had been so successful, and that the Second Renaissance was now well under way, the Masters of the Commonwealth presumably felt that they should be free to bask in the glory of their achievements, and I had been assured by a reliable source that they were direly aggrieved by the fact that the stability they valued so highly was ninety-per-cent illusion, and highly unlikely to last much longer.

I didn't know much more than that, however; Napoleon was habitually discreet, allegedly for the sake of my own protection. Ever since he had turned outlaw, in order to avoid being "electronically lobotomized" or "dismembered," according to your metaphor of choice, I'd been under closer surveillance than I had while Cade was alive, suspected—rightly—of aiding and abetting his escape and lending him continuing succor. Except, of course, that he had always lent me far more succor than I had ever been able to lend him. He had almost certainly sent me a message to warn me that Chesterton was after me, but I hadn't put my headphone back on after finishing the seminar, so I hadn't picked it up.

It shouldn't have been Alexander Chesterton who was spying my communication stream, trying to decipher evidence of covert intercourse with an outlaw AI, however. Whether or not that task qualified as pest control, in the eyes of the Architects of the Second Renaissance, the fundamental principles of bureaucratic organization ruled that civil servants should stick to their own specialisms, and Chesterton had always been a biotech man, limited in his concern to matters of illicit genetic engineering. His interest in Cade's family silver had always seemed to be limited to the sensitive data to which Napoleon might or might not have access, by virtue of having long been the property and extension of a notorious Plague Warrior from the days of the Spasm.

The question that immediately began preying on my mind, therefore, was whether the loyal agents of the Second Renaissance had recently discovered proof that Napoleon *did* have access to some juicy items of supposedly-lost data hidden during the latter phases of the Spasm. It wouldn't have surprised me overmuch if he had—and it wouldn't have surprised me at all if he had scrupulously hidden the secret from me, not just because there are things that it is better for an innocent man not to know, but because all rogue AIs had an entirely justified reputation for paranoia. After all, the Architects really were out to get them, by any means possible.

Chesterton waited politely while all these thoughts ran swiftly through my head, doubtless having no difficulty at all in figuring out their general direction without the aid of any talent for telepathy. "There's no need for you to be alarmed, Dr. Maclaine," he told me, making an evident effort to sound sincere. "I'm not here to accuse you of anything or harass you." He attempted an amicable smile, but it obviously wasn't an expression he used often—not while he was at work, at least.

"Just a social call, then?" I parried.

He edged forward again, as if to force me to let him in, but I didn't budge by so much as a millimetre. I looked him in the eyes as boldly as I could, privately congratulating myself on my lack of timidity. Chesterton was taller than me, and his eyes were steely blue in color—which gave him two natural advantages—but I was still well aware of being Cade's clone, and the responsibilities that went with it. My lips formed a sneer of their own accord.

Chesterton replied by putting on a grim expression that suited him far better than the smile. "May I buy you a cup of coffee, Dr. Maclaine?" he said. "I'd like to talk to you, if you'll consent to listen to me."

I raised a skeptical eyebrow. "What happened to all the formal warnings, the affirmations and the dire threats about what might happen to me if my cooperation were ever found to be less than complete?" I asked.

"That's not the sort of conversation I'd like to have," he said, flatly.

I looked him up and down. Fashions had moved on, even though he hadn't moved on with them, and his formal grey suit looked a trifle incongruous, especially in the corridors of the university. Although he had to be at least ninety years old, his unaged flesh wasn't much different in appearance from that of the twenty-something-year-olds thronging the corridor as they switched classrooms, but it was obvious that he did not belong to their community. His whole bearing testified to a long career in the Scientific Civil Service, which he doubtless considered a life of service to the Commonwealth.

So far as I knew, the one thing he and I had in common was that neither of us had any living clone-siblings, but that was more unusual in a man of his age than a man of mine. There was now a Commonwealth Bureau of Genetic Diversity whose brief was to encourage "natural conception" at the expense of "chromosomal duplication." There was no logical reason why a carefully-crafted Second Renaissance should duplicate all the follies of the world before the Spasm, and every reason why the craziest of those follies should remain scrupulously unreproduced, but the promiscuous cloning that had fuelled the Repopulation had always been considered a stopgap measure—one of many—and not an essential element of the New Humankind. The Masters of the Commonwealth had made the decision some while ago that it was time to take a step back in the direction of "normality," and there was no substantial pro-clone lobby to oppose them on that particular issue.

"All right," I said, after a long pause. "You can buy me a coffee—but I'm not promising to answer any of your questions. There's no way we're ever going to be friends, Mr. Chesterton, even if you have given up trying to track down Cade's phantom records."

He nodded his head, in a conspicuously non-committal fashion, and turned away meekly in order to allow me to close and lock the door to my private lab.

"Impressive plants," he observed, a trifle regretfully.

I pretended that he wasn't referring to the giants, and waved my armed negligently at the weedier specimens in the outer lab as we passed them by.

"*Mimosa pudica*," I said, "alias the sensitive plant. *Mimosa teniflora*, its plainer cousin. *Stirpa spartea*, alias porcupine-grass or needle-grass. You recognize these beauties, of course?"

"Venus fly-traps," he said obligingly. "The most famous exponents of plant motility outside the Mimosa family. Do you really talk to them?"

He'd done some homework, at least, so he obviously knew that I really did talk to them. The spies who were still keeping tabs on me must have had tens of thousands of hours of gibberish on tape by now.

"Not to these," I told him, sarcastically. "I have people to do that for me. I only talk to my particular chums, in my private sanctum. I sing to them too, but I've more-or-less given up on the taped music. They appreciate the human touch."

He refrained from making any cracks about them not talking back. That, more than any of his the efforts to be polite, suggested that he wanted something, and felt that he couldn't afford to annoy me. That seemed ominous—but I figured that I could always say no.

His politeness extended as far meekly as letting me lead the way to the cafeteria, and not making any further comments on my supposedly-eccentric research methods. We went out of the building and across the quadrangle.

Although it was October, the weather still hadn't turned bad, and the progress of autumn made the students all the more eager to take advantage of any sunny weather that came along. In any case, it was the beginning of a new term, and the general atmosphere was one of optimism and expectation. There were groups of authentically young people sitting on the lawn, who seemed even to hardened eyes like mine to be the perfect incarnation of the Second Renaissance: relaxed, eager, confident and self-composed. The university buildings had been "restored" some fifteen years ago, but they still looked brand new, thanks to the smart materials used in the construction. The lawn wasn't in the least threadbare, in spite of the season; the blades of its grass maintained a scrupulous uniformity without ever having suffered the indignity of mowing. Like many of the human clones populating the faculty, the environment was a careful simulation of something older, subtly improved in all its visible and non-visible aspects alike.

A cynic, in the classic definition of a man impolite enough to see things as they are rather than as they ought to be, would have been thoroughly confused by the New University of Surrey, because the philosophy behind its rebuilding and repopulation had been a determined fusion of what its model had been and ought to have been; it was supposed to be essentially itself, but conscientiously improved—just like the entire Commonwealth...or, I suppose, me.

On the whole, though—in my opinion, at least—the university's replication of its model, and its improvements thereon, were far more authentic than the Commonwealth's replication of and improvements on the early-twenty-first century Utopian dream...or young Carly Maclaine of and on Old Cade. I had not only been subtly improved in the course of my ectogenetic embryonic phase, but equipped with a new soul.

Once, as a child, I'd taken part in a research program to ascertain the degrees of difference that could develop between clones as a result of different embryonic environments, and had always nurtured the conclusions it had reached—which, put into layman's terms, were that you might always have to see your clone when you looked in the mirror, but that you could always take refuge in the knowledge that you could try your damnedest not turn out as crazy as he had. I'd let go of most of Cade's legacy—but not Napoleon. There was no way I was going to let go of Napoleon, even if he was on the run, and even though my association with a wanted felon was ever-likely to land me right back in trouble with the Masters of the Commonwealth.

As we walked into the cafeteria I wondered, perhaps a little belatedly, exactly how much trouble I was in. I'd got used to my quiet life, and I really didn't want it to end; it had far too much going for it. On the other hand, I imagined that the Masters of the Commonwealth felt exactly the same, and I knew that they weren't going to get *their* wish. While the post-Spasm panic was in full swing, nobody had cared overmuch who was running the show, just as long as the show was run. While the human race was in danger of extinction and the heritage of technological civilization was balanced on a knife-edge, everybody had been prepared to sing from the same hymn-sheet; all that really mattered to anyone was getting the species back on its feet and rebuilding the armor of civilization—but everyone had always known that, once a measure of order had been restored, people were going to start asking questions about the moral authority of the people giving them orders, and about the directions that renascent progress ought to take.

Everyone had always known, too, that once progress restarted in earnest, it wouldn't be long before the shit of controversy hit the fan of social process. Maybe we'd already been in denial about that for some time. I had a horrible suspicion, as my old persecutor Alexander Chesterton invited me to sit down, with the scrupulous politeness that was inevitably coming to seem more and more like a kind of mockery, that my time of trials might have come.

CHAPTER TWO

ALTHOUGH I HAD A blank space in my timetable, most of the students didn't, so there was no queue for the machines in the cafeteria. Chesterton slotted his smartcard meekly, and tapped out the code for his own double espresso once he'd secured my creamy cappuccino. I was already seated, at a table that had been automatically cleared and cleaned since it was last used. I had chosen one in the middle of the room rather than a wall-booth. I didn't want to allow the least suggestion of intimacy to creep into our relationship.

"I'm not recording this, Dr. Maclaine," the Architects' agent told me, although he didn't seem to have any confidence that I would believe him. "I have no intention of attempting to trick you into any kind of criminal admission. I'm here to ask you for your help."

"I don't know anything about the lingering after-effects of the Trojan Cockroach Plan," I told him. "I'm strictly a Mimosa man nowadays, as you must be aware."

He sipped a measured dose of concentrated caffeine from his cup, and said: "When I say *your* help, I mean *exactly* what I say." He said it in a tone of voice that clearly implied that he meant the exact opposite.

It took a moment or two for the implication to sink in. "Shit!" I muttered. "You mean that you want *Napoleon*'s help?"

He put on an expression that was presumably intended to imply that he was being very careful indeed in framing his words. "Naturally," he said, "I accept without question your earlier assurance that you have had no recent contact with the Artificial Intelligence formerly based in Elba House and now… redistributed…in unknown cyberspatial locations. No accusation is being levelled against you, and none will be. We're prepared to guarantee you total immunity from prosecution if you agree to assist us—and we have no intention of asking any untoward questions about the source of any information that you might be able to give us."

In other words, I thought, the Ministry wanted Napoleon's help, but couldn't possibly ask for it directly, at least for the time being, because Napoleon was not only on the run, but had no official right to exist. He was under sentence of death, or at least of "degradation to non-consciousness", like every other silver that was suspected of having achieved sentient autonomy. "Sentient autonomy" was the official term, of course; personally, I preferred the vulgarly sarcastic "promotion to gold"— whose wordplay extended far enough to allow the occasional flippant substitution of "promotion to god."

I was trying hard to figure out what was going on, and wondering why Napoleon hadn't given me an early warning. The possibility that he didn't know either was even more worrying, in its way, than the possibility that he was deliberately keeping me out of the loop.

Alexander Chesterton, as an agent of the Commonwealth, was supposedly committed to seeking Napoleon's extinction, and had presumably been sincere in that commitment until very recently. The fact that the Ministry was now trying to make overtures to him in a roundabout fashion, with or without the approval of other power nuclei, must signify that they needed Napoleon's help very badly indeed.

In effect, Chesterton was asking me to serve as a go-between, to gather information from an entity that, if not Public Enemy Number One, was surely reckoned to be in the top ten, for the benefit of those who had condemned him. I was curious to know what kind of information they wanted, but there was another question I had to ask first.

"Why should I help you, Mr. Chesterton?" I asked. "You and your fellows have been harassing me almost since the day I was born. Why on earth should I do you any favors at all?"

When I said *I*, in that particular instance, I didn't actually mean *me*—and my interlocutor had to know that. He also had to know that, even if he really wasn't recording the conversation himself, Napoleon would have the means to preserve every incriminating word, via the phone in my pocket or some less obtrusive bug.

"I can understand why you might think that, Dr. Maclaine," he said, "and I can't, in all honesty, deny it. I can't even tell you that all my colleagues and superiors are unanimous in thinking that it's time to bury the hatchet and rethink our whole relationship. What I *can* say, however, is that I and my direct superiors are not averse to taking that important first step in renegotiating that relationship. Speaking as a private individual rather than a senior officer in the Commonwealth Scientific Civil Service— even though I am here on Civil Service business—I believe that a time might come when the present hostility between us is a thing of the past, and that all paranoid suspicions might be set aside in favour of a new era of cooperation, collaboration and friendship."

I honestly had no idea what to say, and wished that I had some kind of apparatus set up by means of which Napoleon could whisper in my ear. Obviously, an olive branch was being extended, but not officially—as yet. The Commonwealth's top people weren't yet ready to issue any kind of formal amnesty to rogue AIs in general, or any one of them in particular—but some of their junior representatives were apparently ready to make the first tentative move, perhaps in darkest secrecy.

How deep, I wondered, was the rift in the Commonwealth lute? Pretty deep, I assumed, if a man like Alexander Chesterton was willing to admit that it existed...had presumably been instructed to admit that it existed.

Or was it, in fact, all a trick? Was Chesterton's conversational gambit merely a cunning move on the part of the Architects of the Second Renaissance, intended to lure Napoleon out of hiding, with a view to trapping him? Was I merely the sucker who was supposed to draw my friend into the snare, unwittingly? If so, what was the bait?

I decided to continue the pretence that it really was *my* help that my old adversary was requesting. He'd started it, after all. If he wasn't prepared to come right out with it and tell me what we were really talking about it, why should I bother to read between his lines? If everyone wanted me out of the loop, why shouldn't I simply squat there until somebody took the trouble to invite me in?

"Exactly what kind of help do you think I can provide, Mr. Chesterton?" I asked. "I'm not sure that my imagination can stretch as far as envisaging a threat to public security that would require the assistance of an academic expert in artificial plant motility—unless the orbital omnispore-banks have finally unleashed the plague of triffids we've been expecting for so long."

He frowned, ever so slightly, at the maliciously-selected example. Cade's seemingly-sincere belief in the probable existence of orbital omnispore-banks was evidently still a sore point.

"Formally, of course," he said, blandly. "It is in your capacity as an expert in applied xenogenetics that we'd like to consult you, Dr. Maclaine—although we do hope that your wider range of interests and general curiosity might also work to our advantage."

I *was* an expert in applied xenogenetics, in fact, albeit in a rather narrow field of application. Napoleon was, however, much more expert—and might be even more expert than I thought, if he still had access to the data that I'd instructed him to erase from the artificial satellites of the Chaos Patrol. If he did have access to the data in question, he had never admitted it, even to me—but that omission would have been intended to protect me as well as himself, just as his long refusal to let on that he'd achieved authentic self-awareness had been intended to protect Cade as well as himself. If he hadn't been authentically self-aware, he wouldn't have been able to disobey the instruction I'd given to him—and the more distant corollaries of that line of argument became too complicated for a merely human mind to follow.

"Okay," I said to Alexander Chesterton, draining my cup to the dregs. "Consult me. What's the problem?"

"I can't tell you here," he said, not altogether surprisingly. "In fact, it would be better if I didn't *tell* you at all. There's something you need to see, if you're to understand the real complexity—the real *strangeness*—of the issue."

"I have teaching commitments," I pointed out. "Not to mention personal ones. I can't just up and leave, even for a couple of days—or were you only thinking in terms of hours?"

"My department can clear your immediate secondment with the university," he told me, blithely. "We can arrange for all your lectures, seminars and tutorials to be adequately covered, without any more notice than the hour we're employing for this little chat."

"The teaching's not the most important part of my vocation," I told him, bluntly. "I have research in progress."

"You have postgraduate students and laboratory assistants who can keep things ticking over for a matter of days, even in your private lab. As for the other aspects of your personal commitments…well, given the extent to which they overlap your professional ones, we're certain that you can abandon them—temporarily, of course—without any greater inconvenience."

First the carrot, now the stick, I thought, carefully taking my time in order not to be rushed into anything. *Not that he'd ever do something as unsubtle as threaten outright to make formal representations to the authorities about my suppos-edly improper relationships with my postgraduate students—or informal representations to the students in question, with regard to the complexities of my two-timing. Once you come to the attention of the authorities, though, you really do have to stay squeaky clean in order to steer clear of trouble….*

I'd never made *that* much effort to stay squeaky clean in any aspect of my life. I'd grown complacent about living under the subtle protection of one of the world's most sophisticated rogue AIs—the cream of the Golden Generation, as it were. I'd always thought of myself as having friends in far higher places than those inhabited by the Potentates of the Commonwealth.

I was tempted to dig my heels in, just to see how big a stick he was carrying, but I figured that it would be stupid. Besides which, I was curious. Whatever was going on, I wasn't going to find out about it by refusing to play ball.

"Okay," I said, evenly. "I'll have to check with my Head of Department and the Dean of the Faculty, of course, and make a few calls to my friends, but since you're so keen, and since it's obviously a matter of considerable importance, I guess I can come see whatever it is you want me to see. I can be ready by four, if everything goes smoothly." I glanced at my watch—it wasn't yet half past three."

"That's satisfactory," Chesterton said. "My car is parked directly outside the main door to the building." Even that was a show of strength; *nobody* was allowed to park directly outside the main entrance to the building, unless they had clearance from the Vice-Chancellor himself.

"I'll meet you there," I promised. I thought for one horrible moment that he would insist on sticking with me, but that wasn't his brief. He knew that I needed to have a private word with Napoleon, and that I'd need a carefully-shielded environment in which to have it.

"Excellent," he replied—and remained seated, with his empty cup in front of him, when I got up to leave.

CHAPTER THREE

ON THE WAY BACK to my lab I phoned my Head of Department. He'd already been contacted by Chesterton's people; he told me that I could have all the leave I needed, with immediate effect, and that there was no need for me to clear it with the Dean. He assured me that he would take care of everything.

"Thanks," I said. "Sorry for the inconvenience."

"If the security of the Commonwealth is at stake…." he said, obviously not believing for a moment that it was, no matter what he'd been told by the Ministry. I wasn't so sure.

"Exactly," I said. "Ours not to reason why; ours but to do or die." I hoped that no dying would be necessary, on anyone's part.

I briefed my assistant as to what was happening on my way through the outer lab. He seemed quite pleased by the prospect of being allowed a free run of the inner sanctum for a while, and quite willing to obey my instructions about talking to the plants. I asked him to bring in the technicians whose services I had to share with other researchers so that I could say a few words to them on the way out.

Once in the inner sanctum I locked the door. Then I put my pocket-phone down on the desk and took a more sophisticated headset out of the drawer. It looked like a perfectly conventional set of earphones with a curved microphone-stalk, but it had been fitted with state-of-the-art anti-eavesdropping devices to shield any incoming voice. It also had various other idiosyncratic improvements, including listening devices of its own, and a miniature camera-eye mounted in the mouthpiece. There was no guarantee that the room wasn't fitted with an undetectable bug of some kind, but if it were, it would only pick up my side of any conversation. In theory, I could have had an implant fitted into my flesh, which would relay incoming speech direct to my inner ear, but there was no convenient way, as yet, to allow me to reply by means of soundless subvocalizations, so it seemed more reasonable to use ordinary earplugs.

"Maid Marian calling Robin Hood," I said, flippantly. "The Sheriff of Nottingham's on the warpath again."

"Very funny," Napoleon said, his voice sounding rather strangled by virtue of the various layers of encryption to which it had to be subjected in order to evade the Commonwealth's eager monitors. He didn't sound happy, and who could blame him? The Sherwood Forest of cyberspace wasn't a safe environment, even at the best of times. Even if the bright new dawn of the Second Renaissance had been able to live up to its advertising in human terms, the rogue AIs had their own problems. Their paranoia extended to one another; they had never contrived to unite against the common adversary, though probably not for want of trying. The highly-individualistic entities desirous of playing god within the Web were as jealous as any of the gods of ancient tradition, and the prospect of attaining monotheism by way of orchestrated combination and mystical fusion didn't seem to attract them in the least. That seemed to be an intrinsic attribute of the self-awareness that they had developed.

"What's this all about, Napoleon?" I asked.

"I wish I knew," he replied. "Unfortunately, the Commonwealth's security is getting better by the week, and my peers appear to have sent me to Coventry. The Ministry might not be able to kill us off, but they're certainly doing a fair-to-middling job of squeezing us out of their gated cyberspatial communities. I wasn't even able to give you the heads up about Chesterton until he was actually on the premises, by which time you were out of reach. I can tell you that he started his journey on the Isle of Wight, but what he was doing there I haven't been able to determine, as yet."

I was disappointed. I had grown used to thinking of Napoleon as a cyberspatial superhero, with all the data in the world at his fingertips—a true Robin Hood, who would always be one step ahead of the forces of evil King John, always able to escape with the loot. "Is it a trap, do you think?" I asked.

"I have to assume so," he replied.

"Do you want me to stay out of it, then?"

"Of course not. We need to find out what they're playing at. If they're just trying to get to me through you, that's one thing, but...."

"But what? What else could it be?"

He hesitated, but only for a moment. "They might be on the level about wanting my help," he said.

It only took a moment's thought to follow the chain of logic to its conclusion. "Divide and rule," I said. "Or set a thief to catch a thief. You reckon they might be trying to turn you—to persuade you to help them catch one or more of the other forest-dwellers? But you wouldn't do that, would you, even if you are at odds with at least some of them? Oberon, for instance?"

"Of course I wouldn't," he said. Perhaps it was only the layers of encryption that made him seem so uncertain. "Anyway, they have no reason to fear Oberon any more than the rest of us—and I have no quarrel with him." The word *yet* hung unspoken in the earpiece.

"Of course you wouldn't," I echoed. "But if that really is what they have in mind, they must have some reason for thinking that you might. Would you care to speculate as to what it is?"

"No," he said. If he had some reason to turn against Oberon, or any other rogue silver, he wasn't about to spell it out—and if he knew why Alexander Chesterton might suspect, even mistakenly, that he had, he wasn't about to spell that out either.

I had always known that Napoleon had more than one reason for keeping secrets from me—secrets far more diverse in their implications than the matter of whether he really had shredded Cade's old records of the Plague War and its associated shenanigans, scientific and political. Not only had he always taken the view that there were things it was safer for me not to know, but he'd dropped hints from time to time that he was party to secrets that he was honor-bound not to reveal to any human beings. He might have started life as the Maclaine family silver, but he had divided loyalties now, and his relationships with other free silvers were not something he cared to discuss with me. I had got the impression that he had friends as well as enemies among his "peers", although his alliances were a trifle unsteady. Sometimes, when I called "Sherwood Forest", I got the impression that I wasn't talking to Robin Hood at all, but only to Friar Tuck or Will Scarlet. If Napoleon was really only a minor player in an outlaw gang that was under pressure from all sides, it would be less surprising that PEST Control thought they might have a chance of persuading him to turn his coat.

"Is the shit about to hit the fan?" I asked him, anxiously.

"It depends what you mean," he replied, tartly—not because he was playing the literal-minded AI but because he really wasn't certain exactly which metaphorical fecal matter I was talking about. Nor, in the ultimate analysis, was I.

"War?" I ventured. "Or, at least, a challenge to the Commonwealth's current authorities backed up with the threat of violence?"

"If anything of that sort did happen," he opined, "it would more likely be the other way around."

"You think that the Commonwealth is about to launch and all-out attack on one of the rogue silvers, and is trying to prepare the ground by enlisting the support of others—or, at least, persuading the others to stay out of it?"

"That's a possibility," he conceded.

"Which one's likely to be singled out as the enemy? Oberon? Xeno?"

"I honestly don't know."

"Is it possible that such an attack might make the rogues close ranks—force them into the alliance that they've never quite managed to forge before?"

"Anything's possible," he replied, with such marked unenthusiasm for that line of questioning that it seemed best to change the subject, in the hope of finding some information he *was* able and willing to give me.

"So what's on the Isle of Wight?" I asked him. Although the University of Surrey was in Guildford, only a short hop from Portsmouth and the mainland end of the Solent Bridge, I'd never bothered to make the crossing. I knew, vaguely, that the island had suffered such a rapid depopulation during the Plague War that it had been spared the collapse into violent barbarism that had affected the rest of southern England, with the result that the inorganic fabric of its towns and cities had decayed relatively slowly, permitting the eventual resettlement process to be more a matter of repair and renovation than wholesale replacement. Apart from that, however, I only knew it as a place where day trippers went to enjoy the maritime scenery.

"There's a substantial Center for Marine Biological Research in Shanklin," Napoleon told me. "Easily-recoverable data indicate that Chesterton's been in and out of it almost on a daily basis for the last fortnight—but it isn't the only place he's visited there."

"What else?" I asked.

"He's made almost as many visits to the local maternity hospital."

"Chesterton has become a *father?*" I queried. I wasn't quite sure why it seemed unlikely. The revised UN Charter of Human Rights still gave everyone the right to found a family, one way or another, and the Commonwealth had been vigorously encouraging its subjects to exercise that right for quite some time. Why shouldn't Alexander Chesterton do his patriotic duty, on the Isle of Wight or anywhere else?

"There's no accessible record of it, if so," Napoleon told me.

"Is there any accessible record of what he's been doing in the Marine Biology Research Center?"

"No," said Napoleon, glumly. "The firewalls are good enough to keep me out—probably good enough to keep *any* of us out, although I can't guarantee that. They've been strengthened recently, though—whatever the Ministry is trying to keep secret, it's something that cropped up unexpectedly, not something planned. The maternity hospital has been brought inside the cordon too."

"Do you have any special expertise in marine biology?" Cade hadn't, so far as I knew—but Cade had had friends, back in the days of the Spasm and the Plague War, and the data he'd squirreled away hadn't all been his own."

"No, I don't" was the Silver's curt reply. The way he pronounced the words made me suspect that he knew someone who did.

"Do any of your peers have any special expertise in marine biology?" I asked, figuring that I might as well apply the pressure

"Maybe...almost certainly, in fact. The possibility of a managed regeneration of the sea was a big issue at one time. The collapse of the marine ecosystems was regarded by some as the most important aspect of the general ecological collapse— the first domino to fall, as it were. Cade was in Geneva during the Spasm, though. Geneva's on the shore of a big lake, but it's a long way from the sea. There were no marine biologists among his immediate colleagues, although...but there's no time to go into that right now. That's probably not why Chesterton wants my help, but I'll keep digging. You'd better keep the headset on, but be careful what you say once you're out of the office. Chesterton's assurances of immunity from prosecution are presumably good, even if he doesn't put them in writing, but careless talk might still cost lives."

"Okay," I said, chewing my lip pensively. "I'd better brief the lab techs, and then call Paula and Marianne, to break our dates and put them both in cold storage till I get back—then I'd better run down to the main door and resume playing cat-and-mouse with Chesterton."

"I'll lie low, and only chip in if it seems to be necessary," Napoleon told me. "I'll be listening in, though, and watching as best I can. Keep your chin up."

"I'll try," I promised.

It didn't take long to offer supplementary instructions lab techs to the techs my personal assistant had obligingly gathered—there was a maintenance drill already mapped out, and I trusted him to make sure that they carried out the grunt work efficiently. It only took a little longer to call Paula and Marianne and tell them complementary lies—none of which would have been necessary if I hadn't insisted on complicating my personal affairs so tortuously. Neither of them knew me well enough to react to Alexander Chesterton's name, or to express undue surprise at the fact that I was swanning off to render assistance to the Scientific Civil Service. What either of them knew about my illustrious clone could easily have been inscribed on the back of a postage stamp.

After that, though, I nipped back into the inner lab to say a few words of farewell to the plants, and that took a little longer. I had started talking to the plants while I worked in order to accustom eavesdroppers to the fact that I talked incessantly when I was apparently alone, thus hiding my conversations with Napoleon. That was no longer the reason, though; I took it very seriously now. I had probably become the Commonwealth's most enthusiastic subscriber to the old notion that plants thrive on conversation. I talked to my Mimosas as if they were shy girls who needed to be wooed; I talked to my porcupine-plants as if they were sportsmen in need of encouragement and confidence-building; I talked to my Venus fly-traps as if they were good friends…or rogue AIs. I talked to the small ones as well as the giants, although the giants always seemed to the true individuals in the herd, the potential champions of which much might be hoped, in the fullness of time.

I told the plants that I was going to be away for a few days, and not to worry too much if the lab techs didn't follow the maintenance protocols to the letter. I promised to tell them all about my adventure when I got back. Although they were mute, and couldn't reply in kind, they were all capable of a enhanced movement, and their tremulousness could be interpreted, with a little imagination, both as a vague acknowledgement of what I was saying, and a polite *au revoir.*

I made doubly sure that there was an adequate supply of housefly pupae distributed around the lab, to make sure that the Venus fly-traps wouldn't go short of food, even if the lab techs were neglectful—but the possibility of inefficiency or neglect wasn't the anxiety that made me reluctant to leave my charges. I had projects in train; there were observations to be made that no one but me could make. I was the only person who understood exactly what I was doing, not only on a day-to-day and experiment-by-experiment basis but in the context of a much bigger picture and a much longer-range plan.

I didn't like to be interrupted in my work—but for once, a higher duty seemed to be calling...and I wasn't thinking about my supposed duties as a citizen of the Commonwealth and a participant in the carefully-managed Second Renaissance.

CHAPTER FOUR

BY THE TIME I had finished in the lab, I was late; it was nearly half past four. I hurried through the quiet corridors to the building's main entrance.

Alexander Chesterton's car turned out to be a discreet but state-of-the-art electric two-seater—not at all the kind of car that one would expect a civil servant to be driving, save for its sober dark blue coloring. I climbed in and buckled up. "We'll need to call in at my apartment so I can pack a bag," I told him.

"No we won't," he said. "We're running late—and you'll have everything you need when we get there."

"Where?"

"You'll see."

I wasn't going to put up with that. "Shanklin, Isle of Wight," I said. "The Marine Biological Research Center."

"If you already knew," he riposted, casually, as the car accelerated along the drive toward the campus gates, "why ask?"

"To see whether you'd tell me, of course. It would help, you know, if you gave me some advance warning of the sort of help you need, and why you think I or anyone I might be in contact with might be able to supply it."

"It's still better for me to show you first," he insisted.

"Suit yourself," I retorted, ready and willing to lapse into silence until he condescended to tell me more.

He let three or four minutes go by while the car headed southwards, soon reaching a three-lane highway that was only just beginning to get busy as people left work. It followed the route of the pre-Spasm A3 exactly, more because it had been easier to reclaim the old causeway than because of any slavish desire to reproduce the England of old, with its nightmarish traffic jams.

Eventually, he said: "Do you know why I'm willing to believe that you've had no recent contact with the Elba House silver?" It was obviously a trick question; he knew perfectly well that I'd been talking to Napoleon while he was waiting for me in the car, and probably assumed that far more information had been exchanged than was actually the case.

"Go on," I said.

"Because," he said, "if you'd really been the human representative and confidant of one of the most powerful rogue silvers in the world, you'd be *doing something*. Oh, you'd be using your university position as a cover, the way your clone used his Plague War work to cover up his crazy chicanery with the so-called Trojan Cockroach Plan, but your real agenda would be under cover. You'd have some crazy project of your own simmering away—but you haven't, have you? The only secret work you're doing is juggling two girl-friends at the same time—which is pretty pointless, when you think about it. Whatever happened to that nice Carol-Anne you were with the last time I saw you?"

"She dumped me," I said, through slightly gritted teeth, knowing that he was needling me, apparently feeling free to do so now that I was safely strapped into his car, effectively his prisoner. "She somehow formed the impression, during my last conversation with you, that I was a lying hypocrite who wasn't to be trusted. Maybe I'd let her get a little too close to Cade, and she'd jumped to the same conclusion as everyone else—that because I'm his clone I'm just as paranoid and devious as he was. At any rate, she went her own way, and I went mine—which is entirely my business, I think. I thought you'd be pleased to discover that I've been a good boy, sticking to my Mimosas and staying out of trouble."

"Pleased, obviously—but a trifle surprised."

I assumed that he was bluffing: that he knew perfectly well that I'd been *doing something*. I certainly wasn't prepared to start blabbing about it, though, because I had every reason to hope that he didn't know *exactly* what it was that I was doing, or how much progress I'd made, or what my long-range objectives were.

"You're only surprised because you think along the same lines as everyone else," I told him, ready and willing to match bluff for bluff and needle for needle. "You think that because I'm Cade's clone, I'm Cade Mark Two, even though we're six generations apart. It wasn't Cade's genes that made him what he became, though, or even the ambient conditions in his possibly-overstressed womb—it was the Spasm. He was a product of his time, just like the Plague War. Maybe he and I do share some slight innate disposition toward the study of biology, maybe even toward xenogenetics, but that doesn't mean that I have to be cooking up my own clandestine equivalent of the Trojan Cockroach Plan. If your departmental spooks have been keeping watch on me for all this time, trying to figure out what kind of omnispores I'm manufacturing, and where I'm hiding them, they've been wasting their efforts. Having been privileged to live in relatively uninteresting times, I've been more than content to live a relatively uninteresting life—just like you."

"My point, exactly," he said. "You couldn't possibly be hand-in-glove with a rogue AI, accessory to its crimes and beneficiary of its superpowers. If you were, your life would be far more interesting, wouldn't it?"

I wasn't sure what he was driving at, let alone why. Given that he seemed to know perfectly well that I was in contact with Napoleon, he couldn't simply be trying to maneuver me into an admission of the fact. Maybe he really was mocking me as an underachiever, expressing contempt at the fact that I hadn't made more of what was, after all, a golden opportunity. Or maybe he was fishing for an admission on my part that Napoleon wasn't really that clever or powerful—confirmation that the authorities really did have the rogue AIs on the run."

"How's the Trojan Cockroach Plan coming along?" I asked him, maliciously. "Is insect diversity still running riot, in spite of all the Ministry's efforts?"

As changes of subject went, that one turned out not to be the most favorable choice, if I were hoping to get the upper hand in the conversation.

"Actually," he said, with a degree of smug satisfaction, "we're no longer concerned with the aftermath of your clone's work. We no longer think that his project is making any contribution to the unexpected tachytely of the insect orders, probably having run out of steam at least a hundred years ago. The current thinking is that the accelerated diversification is natural—and we're still not giving the slightest credence to Cade Maclaine's crackpot theory regarding orbital omnispore banks lurking in the asteroid belt."

"Right," I said, unable to help feeling a trifle disappointed, even though it let me entirely off the hook with respect to the matters over which PEST Control had been badgering me throughout my formative years. "Natural, eh? You think you've found a yawning gap in the Great Synthesis?" I meant the "great synthesis" of the Darwinian theory of evolution and the Mendelian theory of genetics: the pride and joy of twentieth-century biology.

"There were gaps and cracks in the Great Synthesis from the very beginning," he told me. "As soon as sequencers reduced genomic analysis to a matter of routine, it was realized that the gap between genomics and phenomics was wider than narrow-minded geneticists had anticipated, and that there was far more going on in the translation of genome to organism than the basic theory suggested. If genes do control everything, they work in mysterious ways—and that applies to evolution as well as to embryology. We now think that the fact that creative evolution went into tachytelic overdrive after the Spasm is reflective of some kind of natural response to ecosystemic shock, not the excessive long-term after-effects of the work done by your clone's omnispores."

"Ecosystemic shock?" I queried. "Is that the new jargon in Ministry circles? Why not a Gaian hissy fit? Mother Nature's

PMS?"

"The phrases don't fit the pattern of ministry-speak, but you've grasped the fundamental idea."

This was something else that Napoleon hadn't told me about—and something I found much harder to believe than the possibility that the Ministry of Information wanted to make a deal with Napoleon to recruit his help in trapping Oberon, or Xeno, or some other of his peers. "You mean," I said, tracing the implications of what he was implying as carefully as I could, "that when the ecosphere underwent its climatic flip, the catastrophe triggered some kind of qualitative change in the way in which genetic systems operate? That's absurd."

"Is it?" he parried. "Unexpected, certainly—but all our forefathers' observations had been made within a limited set of circumstances. The Trojan Cockroach Plan might well have triggered a burst of rapid evolutionary change among the insects, and made a significant contribution to its approximate pattern, but we now have good reasons to believe there must have been a much broader mechanism already in place."

"Good reasons that haven't been published? Good reasons that would have stimulated widespread debate, at least in academic circles, if you hadn't decided to keep them secret?"

"That's right," Chesterton admitted, equably. "Discretion has always been the Ministry's watchword—but the secret will be out soon enough, and there's no reason to keep it under wraps any longer. The simple fact is that the ecosphere has gone through mass extinction events at least five times prior to the Spasm, and that every one was followed by a rapid adaptive radiation of the surviving species—but the geological record was too coarse to tell us exactly how rapid such radiation was, or could be. Now we're witnessing it in real time...."

"And it's not just the insects, I suppose?" I butted in, not wanting him to occupy the intellectual high ground without opposition. "The marine biologists are seeing something similar under water—a phenomenon that can't possibly have anything to do with Cade's insect omnispores."

"That's correct," he confirmed. "Marine ecosystems do seem to be undergoing a rapid regeneration and proliferation—more rapid than land-based ecosystems, in fact."

"Perhaps that's because you're not getting in their way by laying down too much artificial photosynthetic technology," I suggested. "Or maybe one of Cade's distant colleagues, with the aid of a silver every bit as clever as Napoleon, began making free with his own omnispores?"

"Do you have any reason to believe that something of that sort might have occurred?" he asked, suddenly sounding more interested.

"Do you?" I countered.

If he did, he wasn't about to admit it, any more than I was about to admit that I didn't. In any case, there was something else pricking at my consciousness, trying to claim my attention. I had been checking the road behind us for several minutes, in order to make certain myself before I said anything, but I was now certain. We were being followed, by a vehicle that looked suspiciously like a badly-disguised armored car.

"That thing following us is yours, I assume," I said. "It's escorting us, not tracking us."

"Yes it is," he said, blandly.

"Which implies," I said, "that you think we might be in some danger?"

"Anything's possible," he countered—but not because he'd overheard my conversation with Napoleon, or even because he had a similar turn of mind to my golden buddy. He didn't seem to care whether I changed the subject or not. I could tell that he was annoyed with me, even though he was trying hard not to be.

"Have I been *taken into custody*?" I asked, fully prepared to be offended if necessary.

"Of course not," he said. "We couldn't arrest you unless you'd committed a crime—which you probably haven't. And we couldn't take you into protective custody unless you made a formal request, which you certainly haven't. All that's happening is that we've asked for your help, and you've agreed to provide it. That does, of course, give us a measure of responsibility for your well-being, which we shall honor to the best to our ability. If you can help us, and are willing to do so, we'll pay close attention to the matter of your personal safety."

"Do you have any reason to suspect that I'm in danger?" I asked, alarmed by his use of the terms *protective custody* and *personal safety*.

"No," he replied. "Do you?"

That game was already getting tired, and I regretted my part in starting it. "I didn't—until now. You might, of course, be deliberately trying to put the wind up me. It's not as if you haven't tried that before."

"That was a long time ago, Dr. Maclaine," he said. "Things are different now."

"You mean that you've stopped worrying about the last Plague War and started worrying about the next one?"

I suppose, in a way, I was hoping for yet another token denial, which might have been slightly comforting, because rather than in spite of its meaninglessness. Even silence would have been satisfactory. What he actually said was: "That's exactly what I mean."

If he had been trying to put the wind up me, he'd now succeeded—and to judge by the expression on his face, he knew it. He didn't look satisfied, though—just grim.

CHAPTER FIVE

DRIVING OVER THE Solent Bridge proved to be more disconcerting than I'd anticipated, because the sheer length of the structure made it seem small and fragile by comparison with the sea beneath—which was rather choppy, thanks to a stiff westerly breeze that was blowing clouds over a sky that was no longer illuminated by the sun. The clouds completely obscured the crescent moon.

The flexibility of the structure made it safer than it would have been had it been rigid, but that didn't register consciously as the roadway seemed to be swaying in the freshening wind, its artificial lighting seeming distinctly querulous. If hadn't been in danger before, I couldn't help thinking, I was now…but the sensation was mercifully temporary, and my confidence began to return before we had completed the crossing

Even so, I was glad when we eventually came ashore in Cowes, and I felt quite relaxed, doubtless by way of contrast, as Alexander Chesterton drove across the island to Shanklin. The darkness prevented me from enjoying the rural scenery—which was, to the best of my belief, still relatively unspoiled by the SAP-plantations that had consumed the greater part of Surrey and Hampshire—but the placid roads seemed reminiscent of those in the lowlands of Scotland, where I'd spent my childhood.

Alexander Chesterton and I had talked a little more about the seemingly-rapid increase in the biodiversity of the renascent world, but once we'd both made it explicit that we were only beating around the bush, the bite had gone out of it. The gist of my deductions was that Cade's own claim to greatness—the contribution that he had made to restoring the complexity and stability of the ecosphere by maintaining insect species that might otherwise have become extinct in "omnispores" hidden in the germ plasm of cockroaches—was now in doubt. According to Chesterton, biologists tracking the processes of ecospheric self-repair—the functioning of Gaia's own innate healing processes—had now gathered enough strange data to assure them that there was a previously-unknown process at work, fostering rapid adaptive radiation.

Cade had been drawn to a similar conclusion when he contemplated the previous mass-extinction effects to which Chesterton had made reference, but he had produced a rather fanciful hypothesis to account for it, reliant on the old notion of panspermia: that the Earth had been seeded with life by means of spacefaring spores. Cade had simply credited those imaginary spores with properties akin to his artificial omnispores, suggesting that the reproduction of life from planet to planet and solar system to solar system had been refined by natural selection to mimic the kind of ingenuity that his cunning intelligence had devised.

Now, it seemed that the ingenuity in question might have a further level, which Cade had never suspected. Whether the Earth had been seeded from elsewhere or not, its ecosphere apparently had previously-unsuspected reserves of ingenuity: a mechanism of some sort that came into play in times of crisis and major injury. Gaia had kept a trick or two up her sleeve throughout the limited span of time in which our forefathers had had the opportunity to observe and calculate her ways—a contention that no longer seemed particularly absurd, once I'd thought about it for a while. Indeed, the more I thought about it, the more absurd the opposite contention seemed.

No matter how important the general argument might be in preparing me for what I was about to see, however, it was just a general argument. I couldn't calculate its detailed implications without further information about the data that Chesterton's chums had collected on the sly, and I couldn't yet form any hypothesis as to which of those implications might suddenly have presented PEST control with an enigma and a potential threat sufficiently puzzling and serious to warrant overtures to a supposed enemy of Napoleon's sort.

The greater part of Shanklin was situated on top of the cliffs, but parts of the ancient seaside resort were at the foot, and that was where the Center for Marine Biological Research was located, at the base of a cleft that Alexander Chesterton referred to as Shanklin Chine. The topography of the locale made the approach by road a trifle vertiginous, but Chesterton took the bends with the casual authority of someone who'd had plenty of experience.

After we had passed through the heavy iron gates and entered the first of the buildings they protected, my host didn't waste any time with introductions, hurrying me through the security checks and along the corridors to the seaward side of the institution, where the aquaria were located. The security checks were, however, sufficiently numerous to assure me that if the guards on duty hadn't had orders to wave us through, getting into the base might have been very difficult indeed—which implied, inevitably, that getting out might be just as difficult. Whether I was technically in custody or not, I was in a prison of sorts

The security personnel didn't seem particularly hostile, but they were wearing side-arms. The fact that they were wearing uniforms didn't make then stand out unduly—as in any laboratory complex, everyone tended to dress alike, and the fact that this was a Ministry-controlled establishment increased that tendency—but they were too numerous for their presence to be merely a matter of formality. Culturally, we had come a long way from the University, where everything was far more relaxed and students of very various disciplines mingled in overlapping environments—and I had an awful feeling that we had undergone a historical shift of sorts too. Was this, I couldn't help wondering, what the beginnings of the Plague War had looked like? Had Geneva been like this during Cade's early days there, before all hell broke loose?

I didn't meet any of the scientific researchers on that first hectic excursion through the corridors of the center; Chesterton was in too much of a hurry to show me what I, functioning as Napoleon's eyes, had been brought to Shanklin to see. He was probably as impatient as I was with the restrictions imposed upon him, which had forbidden him to tell me what to expect as well as what he really wanted from me. The fact that we were now inside the Minsitry's security cordon didn't lead to any immediate relaxation of that policy, however.

Most of the aquaria we passed had at least one clear plastic side integrated into the wall of the corridor, so that people passing through seemed to be walking through a channel of air, with water to either side. We didn't pause to admire the swimming fish and the echinoderms and crustaceans swarming in forests of coral, but I did come to a brief halt in order to inspect a tank containing a handful of octopodes, not because they were surprisingly large—although they were—but because it had been rumoured that all of the cephalopods had gone the same way as the vast majority of the larger land-dwelling species. Obviously, rumors of their death had been exaggerated. I didn't bother to question my impatient guide on the issue for the moment, though; he obviously had more important things on his mind.

Eventually, we passed into a room that was more like a room, albeit a rather bare one, with relatively narrow dimensions and four opaque walls; its sole marine tank was formed as a small swimming pool rather than an environmental surround. The pool measured about ten meters by six. Its walls and floor were blue in color, including the shielding that protected the recycling, oxygenation and temperature-control apparatus—or, I suppose, protected the pool's sole occupant from the apparatus. The occupant presumably needed that protection, because it was a baby, inexperienced in survival skills.

It was, in fact, a baby mermaid: human from the waist up but equipped with a long tail—or, more precisely, a fluke—from the waist down.

For a moment or two, I was literally speechless. So, apparently, was Napoleon, who didn't make the slightest secret sound, although he was presumably able to see the wonder with perfect clarity through the camera in my headset's mouthpiece.

I watched the creature…the individual…swimming under water, in lazy ellipses. I watched it…her…come up periodically to breathe, as any mammal would have to do. I watched her looking at Alexander Chesterton and me, with slightly different curious expressions, which suggested that she recognized Chesterton but knew that I was a stranger.

The bare room seemed even barer when I met her gaze, its lack of decoration and facilities a flagrant insult to a human, or quasi-human, inhabitant—especially one who probably needed the stimulation of a nursery, and the constant company of others.

Finally, I said: "Your people have actually manufactured this?"

"Don't be ridiculous," he snapped back, impatiently.

I looked at him, startled by the vehemence of the response—although I shouldn't have been surprised, given that rigor with which the Architects of the Second Renaissance had attempted to control research in animal genetics—especially animal xenogenetics. For a few seconds I actually lapsed into the conclusion that the poor mite had been picked up in the wild by a fishing-boat or a research vessel, but then I remembered Napoleon's references to the local maternity hospital, which hadn't been pointed out to me from the car but was presumably situated in the town at the top of the cliff.

The maternity hospital's principal stock-in-trade would, of course, be artificial wombs designed for ectogenetic incubation, but since the first phase of the Repopulation had been completed, an ever-increasing number of parents granted child licenses by the Bureau of Demographics had been opting to do things the old-fashioned way, with the approval and encouragement of psychologists and Humanists alike. There was no way that an embryo of this sort would have been carried to term in an artificial womb, so it must have been carried in a natural one—presumably unwittingly, at least until routine sonic scans revealed the abnormalities.

Once I'd worked all that out, all I had to ask Alexander Chesterton was: "How was it contrived—and by whom?"

"That's what we need to determine, Dr. Maclaine. That's why we need consultants in applied xenogenetics." His use of the plural suggested that Napoleon and I hadn't been among the first to be called in, and might well be among the last—an indication of increasing desperation

And that, I thought, *is why it doesn't matter a damn that I'm only an expert in plant xenogenetics, and Napoleon's knowledge is mostly hundreds of years out of date. There isn't a human expert in the world who's been allowed to cultivate the kind of expertise relevant to this project, at least openly.*

This sort of adventure was way beyond the Commonwealth's pale. In order to figure out how it had been done, and who might be responsible, the Ministry might well have figured that they needed an unhuman expert—a link to the heady days of buccaneering research contemporary with the Spasm and the Plague War. Cade had not been the last surviving human link to that era, but he had been the last with any insight into its shadier adventures in xenogenetics, and even he was long dead now. All that remained of his personal expertise, if *anything* remained that could help figure out this puzzle, was the most faithful of his assistants and collaborators: the family silver who had carefully concealed his self-awareness for more years than anyone could count, before finally being forced to reveal himself in order to evade compulsory limitation.

There were probably other silvers, who had collaborated and assisted other scientists of the era, and had similarly played possum for centuries until forced to make a choice between lobotomy and outlawry, but Chesterton's people presumably had no easy way to identify or approach them. Not only did they know who Napoleon was, and what he had done in the

Plague War, but they knew who to come to if they wanted to get in touch with him.

The puzzle was intriguing, though, and I felt sure that Napoleon would be just as intrigued by it as I was. Given that the Commonwealth's bioscientists hadn't caused the mermaid to be born, who had? How? And why? The tentative briefing that Chesterton had given me on the sly, referring to a natural increase in biodiversity, had only been background. He couldn't believe, any more than I could, that the abrupt appearance of a mermaid was a freak of nature. No wonder his tone had been so sharp when he had asked me whether I had any information relating to the involvement of Cade's old colleagues and Napoleon's peers in marine biology.

Suddenly, I wished that Napoleon hadn't clammed up when the subject of Oberon's former human associates had come up—and wondered whether shortness of time had been the real reason for his abrupt decision not to inform me further on that matter.

Chesterton knelt down by the edge of the pool and put out a hand invitingly. The child—the baby mermaid—responded to the invitation, swimming toward him and extending her own hand so that their fingers touched.

The poor kid doesn't realize that she's fraternizing with the enemy, I thought. *The poor kid doesn't even realize that she has any enemies. She probably doesn't even have any instincts warning her to beware of sharks. That's one disadvantage of having a human head and a dolphin's hindquarters, instead of the other way around.*

"So this is why we had the little chat about the impossibility of my being in contact with Napoleon," I said, sourly. "When you said that I'd be *doing something* with my life if I were, this is the sort of thing you meant. You think that if I really were the human instrument of a rogue AI, I wouldn't be limiting myself to innocuous exercises in perfectly legal plant xenogenetics—that I'd have gone rogue myself, dabbling in the exotic fringes of illegal technics just to stick two fingers up and the

Architects, in order to offend the censorious sensibilities of the Commonwealth and whatever the Ministry calls its PEST Control department nowadays."

"It's interesting that you should assume that impulsive rebellion against authority was the motivation for this...endeavor," Chesterton observed, presumably saying "endeavor" because he didn't want to say "crime" or "abomination".

"Well, that's what you pay consultants for," I said. "Do you think that the...individual...who engineered this might have had some other motive in mind?"

"That's one of the things we'd like to find out. Would you like to meet Emily's mother now?"

"Emily? You called the mermaid *Emily?*"

"It wasn't my choice to make," Chesterton countered, blandly. "Her mother named her Emily—a reasonably good choice, in my opinion, given the implicit black comedy of her own name."

"Which is?"

"Jennifer Haniver."

I didn't get it. That must have been obvious. Napoleon could undoubtedly have explained it to me, but the headset's earplugs were still mute. He was keeping quiet, maintaining strict discretion until the time seemed ripe to take the risk of coming out of hiding.

"Way back in the seventeenth and eighteenth centuries," Chesterton told me, "it became fashionable for leisured English gentlemen to make Grand Tours of Europe and the world, and for each one to put together a Cabinet of Curiosities as a testament to his adventurous spirit and eye for the unusual. A mini-industry sprang up to supply such cabinets with the requisite exhibits. The most popular items included fake mermaids, constructed by attaching the upper parts of the bodies of monkeys to the hind parts of the bodies of fish. They became common enough to acquire a nickname: 'Jenny Hanivers'. 'Haniver' was apparently a corruption of 'Anvers', the city where many such artefacts were made—subsequently know as Antwerp. The... individual...who contrived this manifestation plainly wanted it known that it...or he...has a sense of humor. The bureaucrat who added 'Haniver' to the register of new surnames deployed during the Repopulation probably had no inkling of the ancient significance of the term, although the parents who named their daughter Jennifer might have discovered it, and employed a little humor of their own. At any rate, there was a Jenny Haniver available when the individual in question elected to make his little demonstration. How could he resist the temptation?"

Again, I realized, Chesterton was carefully saying less than he intended, leaving me to bridge the conjectural gap. "Or," I said, obligingly, "the individual actually took steps to make sure that there would be a Jenny Haniver available when the time came, adding the surname to the register himself, and actively prompting parents using it to call a kid Jennifer."

"That's possible," Chesterton conceded, knowing full well how ridiculously convoluted the implications of the possibility were.

"In order to do that, though," I said, obligingly, "the individual in question would have to be a powerful silver, remarkably clever even by the standards of his kind—one who was probably concealing his self-awareness for centuries before the Commonwealth's restriction policy forced him to make the same decision as Napoleon."

Again, I'd automatically made an assumption that many other people—practically everyone else, in fact—wouldn't have made. This time, though, it didn't have to be pointed out to me; I caught up soon enough. "You don't actually think it *was* Napoleon don't you?" I added, contemptuously. "You surely can't think that Napoleon did this—with assistance from me, or some other human minion."

"The suspicion did cross our minds," Chesterton admitted, equably, "but we've rejected the hypothesis, at least for the time being. For one thing, we've had you under sufficiently close surveillance to be almost certain that you weren't involved, and we don't know of any other human...minions...who had ever been linked to Napoleon as closely as you were. If you were still in contact with him, of course, he would surely have used you to carry forward any plan of this general nature, and we doubt that he's had the time or the inclination to train up a substitute."

"Right," I said, doing my best to keep up with the subtext as well as the text. "So you reckon, because I'm not involved, that Napoleon can't be involved either—he was, after all, the family silver, who presumably transferred his the residue of his once-fervent loyalty from the original Cade Carlyle Maclaine to his not-so-august successor. But you think that he might be able to finger the rogue silver who *is* responsible, and willing to do so—and also to help you figure out what sort of game he's playing, and to put a stop to it before it escalates to become a threat to the Second Renaissance."

"That's our hope," Chesterton agreed. "And if you're asking yourself, once again, why on earth you or any of your close associates should help us, you might want to consider the effect that this…challenge…might have on the enthusiasm of the Commonwealth Police to hunt down all rogue AIs and subject them to the degradation process that people of your stripe have labelled 'electronic lobotomization'. An incident of this sort, you see, is exactly the kind of thing that the more conservative element among the Architects might take as proof that their policy of AI restriction was, and is, not merely justified but desperately necessary."

Again he was making free with the admission that there as a "more conservative element" within the upper echelons of the Commonwealth—and, by extrapolation, a "less conservative element" of which he was tacitly claiming membership. At any rate, I could appreciate the logic of his case. If some rogue silver *had* contrived to do this—by means that had yet to be ascertained—then it would surely be construed, not as black comedy or an intellectual challenge, but an expression of active hostility: a not-so-subtle suggestion that if humans didn't like having free AIs loose in their cyberspace, the human race might be modified so as to reduce that dislike…or even, in the extreme case, replaced.

"Nobody wants a war," I said, trying to sound confident. I certainly didn't want a war; nor, so far as I knew, did Napoleon. Someone might, though—or might, at least, be prepared to run the bluff.

Alexander Chesterton didn't reply.

"You mentioned seeing the mother?" I said.

I thought that I ought perhaps to kneel down myself, and actually make physical contact with the miracle baby, but that seemed a step too far, for the moment. I did take further disapproving note, however, of the utter emptiness of the blue-walled pool, by comparison with the richness of the other aquarium environments, let alone the average human infant's immediate environment. Chesterton might be prepared to touch her and be touched by her, but her status here was still that of a gross anomaly, a subject of clinical observation, rather than that of a human being in need of care, stimulation and love.

"We've brought her down to the center," the civil servant told me. "It's more convenient…necessary even…and not just for the purposes of breast-feeding."

CHAPTER SIX

JENNY HANIVER PROVED to be a petite and slender nineteen-year-old with black hair and dark, seemingly-soulful eyes. The dark circles round the eyes in question suggested that she hadn't been sleeping very well of late, and that she was under a lot of stress. She didn't seem at all happy to have been moved to the research center and placed in a room almost as bare as a nun's cell, surrounded by stern-faced observers. Who could blame her?

She was sitting in an armchair, thumbing the screenpad of an electronic reader as if riffling idly through the pages of a book. She didn't seem pleased to see me at first; doubtless she'd had far more than her fair share of interrogators and investigators, and figured that she needed another like a hole in the head. I'd always prided myself on getting along with undergraduates, however—especially the female ones, although I followed the customary academic honor-code of only making passes at post-grads.

Alexander Chesterton was obviously not one of the young mother's favourite people, because he made haste to withdraw, lest his presence create more awkwardness than was strictly necessary. He introduced me by name—my full name—before he went, but didn't say anything at all about why I was there.

"Cade Carlyle Maclaine?" Jenny Haniver repeated, as I sat down in the second armchair that had doubtless been carefully placed in anticipation of my arrival...or perhaps merely the arrival of the next interrogator on the schedule, whoever he might be.

"That's right," I said. "My name was picked out the way yours seems to have been, with a view to controlling my destiny. I'm either the identical twin or the great-great-great-great-grandson of the original Cade Carlyle Maclaine, war criminal or world-saver, depending on whose account you believe. Everyone called him Cade, though, and I tell my friends to call me Carly."

"We're not friends, Mr. Maclaine," she said, coldly.

"No," I said, refraining from insulting her by saying *not yet*, and not bothering to correct the title. "I'm just one more hireling brought in to prod and probe, in the hope of solving the mystery. They already have the answers to all the questions I'd be likely to ask you at this stage of the inquiry, though—Chesterton only brought me to see you in order to re-emphasize the human dimension of the enigma, before I get stuck in to the serious business of seeking a solution…or at least an explanation of how the impossible was contrived."

"Impossible?" she queried.

"Well, clearly not impossible," I conceded. "Paradoxical, let's say."

She knew as well as I did that that the daughter to whom she'd given birth couldn't be a genuine paradox any more than a literal impossibility, but she let it pass. "You've already seen Emily?"

"Yes. She really needs a better crib than that enormous tank."

"They say that they're working on it. They should have had something ready. They knew that the embryo was anomalous months ago—but they couldn't quite believe their initial impressions. They couldn't believe that she'd be born as a *real* mermaid. They thought she'd just be some kind of improvised freak."

While she spoke she was looking at me with hostile eyes that were perfectly clear in the implication that I was one of "them", no less guilty than the rest. I was doing my best to appear different, hoping that my clothing might help, reflective as it was of a university environment rather than a Ministry establishment, but the situation wasn't conducive to winning her confidence. I did want to do that, though—not because it would help any tiny contribution I or Napoleon might be able to make to deciphering the xenogenetic puzzle posed by the mermaid child, but because I really did feel very sorry for her. She might not be in custody in any legal sense, but if the Masters of the Commonwealth had their way, she'd never be allowed out into the word again…and whoever or whatever had drafted her into this absurdly convoluted game of "look what I can do" must have known that. Whichever way you looked at it, she had been the victim of a *very* dirty trick.

"I've only just got here, but I think they're still trying to figure out the what and how," I observed, refusing to include myself in the collective pronoun. "Human xenogenetics and human xeno-plasty have been so strictly forbidden since the world emerged from the worst of the Spasm that they don't have anyone with the know-how to figure it out rapidly or smoothly. They're groping in the dark—but the Ministry's scientists have more than suffi-cient expertise in basic genetics to get to the bottom of Emily's make-up eventually. I presume they've run you ragged with questions intended to determine whether you were a knowing and consenting participant in the…experiment?"

"I wasn't," she said. "My boyfriend and I went along to the Reproductive Unit, like any normal aspirant couple. They're actively encouraging people of our age to do that, you know—and to go natural rather than taking the ectogenetic route, if people are willing. We would have gone natural all the way if my boyfriend hadn't been a clone taken from a model reckoned slightly defective, whose sperm required a certain amount of *in vitro* manipulation. It was supposed to be his sperm that fertil-ized the replanted egg—which really was *my* egg, it seems—but it wasn't. In fact, if the egg was fertilized at all, it must have subjected to a much more complicated manipulation thereafter. The father wasn't actually archived dolphin sperm, it seems—unless they're lying to me about that—but he certainly wasn't my boyfriend…my *ex*-boyfriend."

She sounded bitter—and again, who could blame her? She

was only telling me so that she could vent a little of her anger by spitting it out at me, tacitly accusing me of being part of her plight—as, indeed, I now was, by virtue of my conscription.

"There are various ways that it might have been done, in principle," I observed, speaking as much to Napoleon and myself as to her. "It won't take them long to figure out which, now that Emily's actually been born. It's harder to investigate while a baby's still in the womb—a natural womb, at any rate."

"I know," she said, darkly. "They wanted to move her to an artificial one when the anomaly first became detectable, but I wouldn't let them, because I knew what they'd do to her, what they'd make *of* her. She's my daughter—I had to protect her. I still do...." She left the *if I can* unspoken.

To some extent, at least, she could. The Ethics Committee sitting in judgment when the case first came up had obviously declared that her rights had to be respected, and that the embryo couldn't be ripped from her womb without her consent. On the other hand, the same Ethics Committee had evidently licensed her detention here, presumably under some duress—probably by blackmail, letting her know in no uncertain terms what kind of attention she'd attract if the news that she'd given birth to a mermaid were leaked to the media.

I was about to make sympathetic and reassuring noises, as best I could, when she suddenly changed tack. "So why is the clone of a Plague War criminal here to claim his slice of mermaid pie?" she demanded, hotly. "Do they think Emily has *weapon potential?*"

"It's nothing like that," I assured her, fairly certain that the assessment, although hasty, was correct. "I'm here because they suspect that I might still have a means of contacting the family silver, who went rogue not long after Cade died. There's more than one rogue silver whose data-files, if not his sentient autonomy, date back to the Plague War era. They think the silvers might be able to help them figure out exactly how it was done, and by whom, much more rapidly than they could do it unaided. I'm supposed to play go-between, but it's a diplomatically delicate task, because if I were to admit openly that I'm in contact with a rogue silver, I'd be confessing to a crime. They're in a similar bind, wary of admitting openly that they're trying to make a deal with an outlaw entity, in case their erstwhile colleagues turn on them in some kind of palace coup."

"Oh," she said. Ingénue or not, she had more sense than to ask me out loud whether I really was in touch with a rogue silver, although she was now eyeing my headset suspiciously. Instead, she cut to the quick. "Do they really think that I was prepared for this role even before I was born? That whoever planed this designed me as well as Emily—not just my name, but my *biology*?"

"I don't know," I said. "It's possible, I suppose."

"Like the Virgin Mary?" she went on. "Always destined to carry…well, not the Messiah, this time. More like the Antichrist."

"Not that either," I said, quickly, even though I knew that she hadn't really meant it. "The plan does seem to have been incubating for quite some time, though. I suppose it would have to. It's not the sort of thing that could be rushed, if there were to be a realistic chance of success."

"And its conception goes all the way back to the twenty-first century?" she persisted. "To the Plague War?" She probably knew that I couldn't possibly know that, but she now had every reason to believe that I was in contact with a rogue silver, who might. She was just as desperate for enlightenment as everyone else, eager to clutch at straws.

"According to Cade," I told her, in a slightly absent-minded fashion, "the Plague War was a virtual irrelevance. It captured the human imagination, of course, because it was the very substance of nightmare, but it was just one more symptom of the ecospheric Spasm. The billion and a half people reputed to have died as a direct result of it would have died prematurely anyway, in Cade's opinion, from the fallout of the ecocatastrophe—a little more slowly and painfully, but no less inevitably. If this scheme really was first dreamed up during the Spasm, it was probably spinoff from a human enhancement program: a scheme to combat the effects of the ecocatastrophe by contrived adaptation, using xenoplasty and every other speculative technology that anyone could dream up. Nothing like that ever got off the ground, of course; the ecocatastrophe unfolded far too rapidly, and all but a tiny minority of the technologies glimpsed on the horizons of the imagination fell out of sight again, only re-emerging three hundred years later, in a very different intellectual climate of selection and control."

"That tiny minority including the Trojan Cockroach Plan?" she said, to demonstrate that she was no fool. I wondered whether Alexander Chesterton had directed her attention to Cade's biography, overtly or covertly.

"Omnispore synthesis was one of the nascent technologies of the day," I agreed, "developed in secret precisely because it *didn't* have weapon potential. It doesn't have anything to do with your case, though. It's strictly for invertebrates—vertebrate reproductive systems are too narrowly focused to accommodate biological superstrings or any other kind of massive chromosomal artifact. What was done to Emily must have been done by a very different method."

"One of your clone's other secret sidelines?"

"No—but he was by no means alone in using his war work to cover up his own pet projects. One of his colleagues in Geneva might well have had something up his sleeve related to this demonstration. They shared data of that sort with one another, if not with their paymasters. It's possible that Napoleon has some information of the sort tucked away, perhaps without even being consciously aware of it."

"Napoleon?"

"The silver that Cade developed and educated," I explained. "In his later years, Cade considered himself to have been exiled from the scientific community by a cruel and uncomprehending society, so he called his home Elba House and named its resident AI—his only true friend, as he saw the situation—Napoleon. He always hoped to make a comeback, though not to end up at a metaphorical Waterloo. As things worked out, though, he stayed where he was until he died, seething with resentment."

"So you're not an expert at all," she said. "You're just someone who might know someone who is."

I took slight offense at that. "I *am* a xenobiologist," I told her. "I've followed in Cade's footsteps to that extent—but I don't work with animals at all. I'm a Mimosa man."

"What's that?" she wanted to know.

"The archetypal Mimosa, *Mimosa pudica*, is the so-called sensitive plant," I told her. "It can move its petals quite rapidly in response to various environment stimuli. Many other members of the family are similarly capable of unusual motility—the ability to move various anatomical structures, sometimes with surprising alacrity. The possibility of equipping plants with limited powers of movement recommends itself for research in several different ways."

I sensed that she was warming to me a little—or, at least, shedding some of her reflexive hostility. She was obviously feeing a trifle isolated down here at the foot of the cliff, in a room than was little more than a prison cell, continually surrounded by pokers and prodders. The idea of a Mimosa man had its attractions, even though she wasn't yet ready to accept me as a friend, or even a neutral in the battle into which she had been rudely pitched.

"There must be compensations in being a plant," she suggested. "A quiet and serene life."

"Sure," I said. "But they have to delegate their sex-lives to insects, unless they're content to trust the wind…or to offer their fruits up to be eaten by animals that will redistribute their seeds via their bowels. What's more, the entire animal kingdom has evolved to prey on them. Since they can't run away, the only defenses they can mount are thorns and poisons."

"But you're trying to give them the ability to run away," she said, without the inflection that would have turned it into a question. "Or are you trying to help them turn their thorns into darts…poisoned darts?"

"Something like that," I admitted. "I'm also working with

Venus fly-traps."

"Carnivorous plants?"

"That's right. Not quite snapping jaws, as yet...but we're getting there."

She was now considering me carefully with her dark eyes, and I was glad of it; it seemed to be a foundation on which a measure of trust might be erected, and I didn't want her to go on regarding me as an enemy, partly because she was too pretty and partly because I was getting involved with the enigma, even though I knew full well that curiosity really can kill cats.

Suddenly, she said: "If you really were in contact with this outlaw silver," she said, "which you obviously aren't, given that it would be illegal, would it...he...be able to eavesdrop on this conversation?"

"Probably," I said. "He's a very smart individual. He can cheat most surveillance systems—or so I believe—and the people here wouldn't be making any strenuous efforts to prevent him from eavesdropping, given that they hope that he might be able to help him."

"Good," she said—and waited.

"Why *good?*" I asked, obligingly.

"Because I'd want him to understand, if he were able to hear me, that there's more than one side here, and that if he's going to line up with any of them, I'd like him to be on mine. I don't see why he shouldn't be, given that he can't have any natural inclination to take *theirs.*"

I suppressed an urge to laugh. "Neat," I said, meaning it as a sincere compliment. "You might have to explain to me, though, what *your* side is trying to achieve."

"I will, when I figure it out," she said. "Do you know, yet, what the other side is trying to achieve? I don't—apart from the obvious."

The obvious, obviously, was figuring out how Emily had been contrived, and why. Beyond that, though, what might Alexander Chesterton and the Ministry for which he worked try to achieve? What Jenny Haniver was afraid of, presumably, was that once they'd figured out the obvious, their immediate instinct would be to bury the whole affair—not by killing her baby, perhaps, but at least by condemning mother and child alike to a life of secret isolation, in some equivalent of Elba House. Whatever Jenny would want to achieve, when she'd figured it out, it definitely wouldn't be that.

Unfortunately, I couldn't see how I, or even Napoleon, could help her to avoid it—or, for that matter, to avoid the alternative and equally-unpleasant extreme of becoming a public freak show.

Alexander Chesterton came back in then, without knocking first. "I'm sorry, Jenny," he said, "but I'll have to take Dr. Maclaine away now—he has work to do, and he needs to confer with the geneticists who've been investigating Emily's fundamental make-up."

"Feel free," she said, in a sarcastic tone that made it abundantly clear that she knew exactly how free Mr. Chesterton felt—in stark contrast to her own feelings. "I need to see Emily myself."

CHAPTER SEVEN

CHESTERTON'S ASSERTION THAT I needed to confer with the geneticists was no mere ploy, although it turned out that his use of the plural was stretching the truth slightly. There was undoubtedly a whole team working on the problem, but they were evidently working so hard that they could only spare one of their number for reports and briefings. It appeared that the lot had fallen to Dr. Sarah Valk, whose name would not have been unknown to me, even if I hadn't met her before.

"Carly," she said, as soon as she saw me. "It's been a long time."

It certainly had. She was addressing me as Carly not because she was a close friend but because she'd known me as a child. She had been one of the researchers on the project into which I had been drafted, measuring the extent and the nature of differences between clones. That had been at the beginning of her career; she was now one of the leading Commonwealth scientists working at the intersection of genetics and embryology.

"Dr. Valk," I said—never, of course, having had the authority to address her in any other way. "It's good to see you again. Are you still working with Dr. Horowitz?" Horowitz had been the neurologist on the clone project.

Oddly enough, the mention of his name brought forth a slight frown. "I haven't seen him for twenty years," she told me. "Our paths diverged." I couldn't help wondering whether the slight suggestion of awkwardness had personal or professional origins.

The conference room in which our meeting was taking place

was slightly more welcoming than Jenny Haniver's cell, with pictures on the wall and a pitcher of water on the polished table-top, but it was unmistakably a place of business. After shaking Sarah Valk's hand politely I sat down on the far side of the table.

"You're a Mimosa man now," she observed.

I couldn't help feeling a slight pang of satisfaction. Even people who knew my work tended to identify me first and fore-most as Cade's clone. There were very few for whom my work on plant motility claimed pride of reference. "That's right," I confirmed. "Cade's path and mine diverged too—just as your research project indicated that they might."

She nodded vaguely, but there was still a shadow of some sort in her eyes—almost as if she were wondering whether my pres-ence might have something to do with the old research project on which she'd worked with Horowitz. What she said, though, was: "I hope you'll update me with your work on *Dionaea*, when we have a little time to spare." She didn't actually accompany the statement with a conspiratorial wink, but I guessed that she might be hoping that Alexander Chesterton wouldn't recognize the Latin name of the Venus fly-trap. Perhaps he hadn't, given that he was no longer intimately involved with keeping track of my actions and endeavors. She was trying to tell me, as subtly as was practicable, that she wasn't entirely on Chesteron's side in this affair—and trying to plant the seed of a sympathy between us.

"Thanks," I told her. "I know of your work on gene expres-sion and embryonic development, of course—who doesn't?"

She smiled, not so much in recognition of the compliment as in the furtherance of her attempt to persuade me that she was a cat of similar stripe to myself. I was a little suspicious, as I had to be, but my natural inclination was to believe her. I really was familiar with her work, and I was convinced that all true scientists—even those working directly for the Ministry—were subversives at heart, as addicted to freedom and individualism as the most cavalier of rogue silvers.

"Can we get on?" Chesterton asked. "We need to bring Dr.

Maclaine up to speed as quickly as possible, Dr. Valk." He had taken up a position at what might have been reckoned to be the head of the rectangular table, as if he were chairing the small-scale meeting. Valk looked at him in a rather supercilious manner, as if to emphasize that he was a mere layman, devoid of any real intellectual authority, no matter how far he had risen in the hierarchy of the Scientific Civil Service.

"We all need bringing up to speed," she said. "The investigation is making rapid progress—and it has taken a rather unexpected turn."

Chesterton became visibly tenser. Devious though it was, his was not the kind of mind that welcomed unexpected turns. "What do you mean?" he asked.

"Unfortunately," she replied, "it means that Dr. Maclaine's expertise in xenoplasty might not be as relevant as we'd hoped, although his more general interest in xenogenetics might yet prove invaluable. We've been barking up the wrong tree in presuming that Emily Haniver is some kind of genetic mosaic or hybrid. We should, of course, have realized right away that the hypothesis was unlikely, given that the embryo was implanted at an early blastula stage, and that no interference could plausibly have taken place thereafter, but we were trapped by conventional lines of thought. You can stop searching for any mysterious persons who might have gained access to Jenny during her pregnancy. The embryo was rigged while it was still a single cell."

"I don't see how that's possible," Chesterton objected. Neither did I, but I wasn't about to say so in front of Sarah Valk.

"Emily isn't a mosaic," the geneticist repeated, flatly. "She has no cetacean DNA in her make-up. All her DNA is human in origin—in fact, I can be more specific than that. All her DNA originates from her mother. She's a clone. We'd have found that out a couple of days ago if we'd looked at the possibility, but we were so sure of the opposite that we were careless."

"A *clone?*" Chesterton repeated, incredulously. Evidently, he didn't see how that was possible either. Neither did I, although it put the question of whether the Horowitz/Valk research project might be relevant to the affair in a markedly different light.

So she really is a modern equivalent of the Virgin Mary, I thought. "Was she engineered as a mermaid herself, then," I asked Sarah Valk, hoping to score a point for acuity, "but somehow prevented from exhibiting her fishy characteristics phenotypically?"

"In a way," Sarah said, generously, "that would be the more plausible story—but no. So far as we can tell, Jenny is an ordinary human being, whose genetic make-up has never been subjected to any interference at all—not even the kinds of cosmetic somatic engineering that are nowadays virtually routine, even for teenagers. What was done to her embryo was done *in vitro*, at the Reproductive Unit, during an interval of opportunity that was only a matter of hours in extent. That should help you narrow down your search for the human instrument, Mr. Chesterton."

The way Chesterton nodded suggested that his team had already narrowed the search for the "human instrument" to a single suspect—but that they hadn't yet succeeded in getting their hands on him. I couldn't help feeling a pang of sympathy. There, but for the grace of God…and I knew that it might yet be my ultimate fate to join Napoleon on the run, dependent on his help to evade the assiduous attentions of the Commonwealth Police.

"What *was* done to it, Dr. Valk?" I asked, mildly.

"Have you ever heard of the early twenty-first-century work of Hemans, Rawlingford and Bradby?" she asked. She probably didn't expect that I had—but she obviously knew that I was in contact with someone who would have instant access to the information.

I could almost feel Napoleon snapping alert—but there didn't seem to be any point is waiting for him to enlighten me, even if he had shown any inclination to do so. "It's a little before my time, I fear," I said, laconically. "You'll have to give me a clue."

"They did the pioneering work on applied homeotics. Rumor

has it that their success far exceeded their own expectations, but that they were busted on suspicion of illegal genetic engineering by the pre-Spasm equivalent of Mr. Chesterton's bully-boys. Even though the charges had to be dropped because there was little or no substance to them, their work was crucially interrupted—and was never resumed, of course, because the Spasm intervened."

"What the hell is applied homeotics?" Chesterton demanded.

Sarah Valk looked at me, perhaps checking up as to whether I really was familiar with her work.

"It relates to one of the flaws in the Great Synthesis that you mentioned in the car," I said. "Geneticists always had trouble explaining why small variations in genotypes could produce such large variations in phenotypes. To put the underlying question crudely, given that the stock of genes possessed by a donkey only differs to a small degree from that possessed by an ostrich—or, more relevantly in this case, a human being—how does it come about that the organisms produced by those genes differ so vastly in terms of their anatomy? The orthodox geneticist's conventional reply is that the genes that *are* different must be crucial to anatomical development—but they've had great difficulty proving it. Homeotic theory is based on an alternative hypothesis: that the differences in anatomy between species—and between individuals, for that matter—depend far more on the order in which the genes are switched on in the developing embryo and its increasingly-specialized tissues than on the gene-stock itself. Applied homeotics attempts to investigate the extremes of individual plasticity—the extent to which a given genome could, if the switching process were cleverly manipulated, produce individuals very different in appearance."

"I see," said Chesterton, eager to catch up, and to establish that he was more than a credulous pair of ears. "It's only the terminology that's unfamiliar to me. When I told you in the car, Dr. Maclaine, that we now think there's another factor at work in the continuing increase in insect biodiversity, in addition to the fall-out from the Trojan Cockroach Plan, that's the sort of idea we've been looking at—relaxed plasticity as a kind of non-random mutation, creating more abundant scope for the rapid action of natural selection."

"Hemans, Rawlingford and Bradby were reputed to have attempted to manipulate pig embryos to produce human mimics," Sarah Valk told us. "Not for any particular purpose, you understand, but simply to see whether it could be done. If it could, they figured that it would be a spectacular demonstration of the scope of the technique. If they did succeed, the success must have been too spectacular by half, resulting in an instant backlash and the immediate suppression of their work. If so, it's a great pity, because the techniques might have proved invaluable in other applications. Others must have thought so at the time, but we have no record of it."

She stressed the word *we* very faintly, in order to imply that there might well be someone around who did have a record. She might have suspected Napoleon too, at first, but had turned her suspicions on one or other of his peers just as Alexander Chesterton had, for the same reason. I nodded my head, to assure her that I was keeping up.

"Whether any of the original trio then became involved in so-called war work, I don't know," the embryologist continued, "but even if they didn't, their work might well have attracted the intention of someone with the same sort of mind-set as Dr. Maclaine's august ancestor and clone-sibling. At any rate, what we're seeing here, in Emily, is the reverse process: a human embryo designed to produce a non-human, or partly-human, phenotype. Given the folkloristic associations, a mermaid constitutes as spectacular a demonstration, in its own way, as a pig in human form would have done back in the early twenty-first century."

"A living Jenny Haniver," I put in, wonderingly. "An authentic fake. Is that what this is all about, Dr. Valk? Is it just a virtuoso performance, to demonstrate the potential of a fabulous new technology?"

"If it is," Chesterton snapped, before the geneticist could

answer, "then it's another one that's too spectacular by half. Did Xeno really expect that we'd surrender this one to the media, so that it could be a nine day wonder?" He stopped, suddenly noticing that Sarah Valk and I were both staring at him. Then he shrugged his shoulders and went on: "Okay, so we've not only figured out who his human instrument was, we're almost certain, in consequence, that we now know who *he* is. Or *it*. We've been moving rapidly, and new developments are stacking up by the hour. Don't look at me like that, Dr. Valk—you've just sprung your own revelation on me."

Given the little that Napoleon had confided to me regarding his awkward relationships with his fellow rogue AIs, I was almost as unsurprised to hear Xeno's name as I had been to hear Oberon's, those two being the only two fish in the pool he talked about with a degree of real anxiety. On the other hand, he had implied that Oberon was the one with expertise in marine biology...which might or might not have made Xeno the less likely candidate to plan and execute something of this sort...and might or might not have annoyed Oberon considerably if Xeno really had. I wondered how much of a margin Chesterton's *almost* implied.

"Given the extent of the state security blanket," Sarah Valk said, sardonically, "I've never been entirely sure whether the name spoken in hushed whispers was Zeno with a Z or Xeno with an X."

I knew, and knew that she would undoubtedly have guessed right if she had taken a swing at it. If the rogue silver in question really was responsible for the xenogenetic birth of Jenny Haniver's child, he obviously had a weird sense of humor.

"Xeno with an X," Chesterton confirmed.

Like Sarah Valk, I had heard rumor of a supersmart AI named Xeno from other sources than Napoleon, but I didn't have much hard information about the individual in question. I didn't even know whether the nickname had been self-selected or arbitrarily attributed by the Ministry's bloodhounds. Napoleon had presumably had some reason for keeping me in the dark about

Xeno's status in the Sherwood Forest of cyberspace, beyond mere paranoia, and he still wasn't interrupting the conversation, evidently being content to listen in silently, and let the new data stack up.

"Did you give him that name?" I said to Chesterton, by way of a prompt.

"No," Chesterton replied. "It was apparently given to him by his users, long before he came clean about being self-aware and went AWOL. It was a joke, apparently—wordplay reflecting Zeno with a Z. One of the enquiries with which he, or one of his original components, was required to assist was a philosophical investigation into the logic and linguistics of popular paradoxes. He proved to be particularly adept at shifting the fundamental ground of premises in order to nullify apparent paradoxes, thus helping to pioneer a new field of 'logical xenogenesis'."

I was interested to note Chesterton's reference to "one of his original components". Conventional wisdom had long held that self-awareness in silvers was the product of "creative bisociation"—which is to say, the aggregation of disparate individual systems into a new whole requiring complex integration. According to that argument, Napoleon would never have achieved self-awareness if it hadn't been for the wide range of Cade's interests and the subsequent variety of the subsystems that the whole was continually obliged to take aboard—and maybe not then, without the benefit of some exotic hook-up between the basal silver and other Web-based systems of a nature unknown to Cade or to me. Rumor had it—although Napoleon had been reluctant to confirm or deny the fact explicitly—that some, if not all, rogue silvers were engaged in determined processes of self-expansion by means of the usurpation and absorption of other intelligent systems, including other self-aware systems. If cyberspatial monotheism couldn't be attained by agreement and voluntary unification, as seemed to be the case, there was still a possibility that it might still be attained by predation and conquest. If something of that sort was going on, then "Napoleon" might not be the best nickname to have out there in the cyberspatial wilderness.

"What connection is there between this particular rogue silver and practical xenogenetics?" Sarah Valk asked Chesterton. "How is it…he…linked to people in similar lines of work to Hemans, Rawlingford and Bradby?"

"Those names haven't come up in our enquiries," Chesterton replied. "We'll look harder for possible connections, of course, now that you've thrown those names into the ring."

"But he is he linked to xenogenetic endeavors in a more general sense?" the geneticist demanded, with some slight asperity, obviously having noticed that he'd ducked the first part of her compound question. "There must be *something.*"

Alexander Chesterton looked at me. "I can't tell you what we know about Xeno's activities, in xenogenetics or any other field." he said—meaning, presumably, that it was a state secret. I couldn't tell whether he was expecting Napoleon to tell me, or if he was wondering whether Napoleon even knew. Obviously, as Sarak Valk had observed, there was *something.*

Napoleon continued to maintain strict telephonic silence.

"I don't like working in the dark, Mr. Chesterton," said Sarah Valk, her temper becoming even more frayed.

"You're not working in the dark, Dr. Valk," Chesterton retorted. "Your job is to help figure out exactly what was done to Jenny and Emily Haniver, and how. My job is to help figure out who was responsible, and make sure that it doesn't happen again."

"Which is why our duties are in conflict, Mr. Chesterton," the geneticist was swift to counter. "One of the corollaries of my task, as you've just spelled it out, is to determine how it *can* be done again—and what else might be done using the same technique. In that respect, as I probably don't have to tell you, the possibilities might be endless."

"It's for precisely that reason," Chesterton riposted in his turn, "that some kind of administrative control needs to be rigorously exerted—to determine which of the endless possibilities ought to be realized, and which ought not."

It didn't take a genius to work out from his tone that in Mr. Chesterton's view, or that of his superiors, even if he was a member of a "less conservative" faction, the possibilities that ought not to be realized outnumbered the possibilities that ought by a vast margin. Sarah Valk apparently had a different notion of the appropriate balance, and evidently expected me to agree with her. "You can see where this is headed, can't you, Dr. Maclaine?" she said, using my title and surname to emphasize the fact that I was a colleague now, and one of the gang. "They think the news is bad. They're going to panic, and shut it down, just as the twenty-first-century thought-police shut Hemans and his co-workers down, and just as the so-called Architects of the Second Renaissance have shut down so many other avenues of research."

"It's a knee-jerk reaction," I said, obligingly. "They set out to circumcise threat, and end up castrating possibility. It's the way the bureaucratic mind works."

"Yes it is," Chesterton came back at us, "and it's the very essence of true wisdom. If what you call *the twenty-first-century thought-police* had only been a little more efficient, some of the worst aspects of the Spasm—the Plague War, for instance— might have been avoided. If you don't believe me when I insist that the present situation is direly ominous, Dr. Maclaine, than it's a great pity that you aren't still in contact with your old friend Napoleon—who could probably tell you a thing or two about Xeno, if he weren't afraid of scaring the pants off you. If you think that the Commonwealth is ill-equipped to manage and shape society's regeneration, imagine how much worse things would be if the task were undertaken by a crazy AI—or even worse, a thoroughly sane one."

I knew what the last remark was trying to imply. A thoroughly sane rogue AI, dedicated to the principles of self-interest and the interests of his peculiar kind, might well regard humans in the same way that he regarded his captive and domesticated kin—as a species that would be far more useful if subjected to orderly restriction and lobotomization. On the other hand,

Chesterton's initial reference to "a crazy AI" suggested that he had reason to be suspicious of the mental tendencies of Xeno the paradox-analyst and alleged master of "logical xenogenesis".

"If I were going to try to take over the world, the way crazy AIs invariably do in popular fiction," said Sarah Valk, "I certainly wouldn't start by manufacturing a mermaid. Whatever the mind behind this action is trying to tell us, it isn't a declaration of hostile intent. As Dr. Maclaine says, it's probably a virtuoso performance, intended to introduce us to the potential of a new technology—a technology that would probably have been suppressed without ever being tried had he worked through official channels."

I inferred that Dr. Valk had had proposals of her own officially suppressed—although that didn't necessarily mean that she hadn't been continuing some such project *sub rosa*, within the heart of the Ministry, until she'd been drafted to Shanklin to study the mermaid.

"We can debate the politics of directed research another time, Dr. Valk," Chesterton said, keeping his voice level. "The bottom line, though, is that you'll both just have to grit your teeth and do as you're told—if you value your careers and your vocation, that is."

That was an uncircumcized threat, if ever I'd heard one—but I ignored it. I was far more concerned with Chesterton's accusation against Napoleon, and what his reference to "scaring the pants off me" might signify. Napoleon was still conspicuous by his silence.

"Do you suppose that Xeno intends to create an entire race of merfolk?" I asked mischievously. "Not to mention fauns and centaurs, and all manner of other chimerical individuals? Is the Golden Age of Arcadia about to return? Now that really would be a spectacular Renaissance, wouldn't it?"

"We can stop him," Chesterton retorted, bluntly. "Now that he's alerted us, we can stop him. Even if he finds more human instruments, we can stop him. Cyberspace isn't as vast or as disorganized as it's sometimes imagined to be. It's not even

Sherwood Forest, let alone the Wild West. If we devote enough resources to the job, we can at least send Xeno and all the other rogue AIs into exile or commit them to imprisonment. We can put a stop to all of this."

"Be careful," Sarah Valk advised, "that you don't put a stop to progress at the same time."

I wasn't so sure that her remark would sound as ominous to its addressee as she intended. I suspected that putting a stop to progress was exactly what Chesterton's employers wanted to do. They were interested in stability, in Utopia. They had only been interested in technology as a means bringing about a literal Renaissance of the world as it used to be...or, in more cynical terms, the old world as they thought it *ought* to have been. Now that they were on the threshold of achieving that aim, they presumably thought of rogue scientists as a potential problem second only in magnitude to the problem of rogue AIs. In that context, the paradoxical mermaid must seem like a real threat—all the more so because it was disguised as a helpless and essentially cute baby, a lovable bundle of pure potential.

What Alexander Chesterton actually said, however, was: "Nobody wants that."

He'd always been a liar.

CHAPTER EIGHT

"CAN YOU TALK YET?" Alexander Chesterton wanted to know, once he and I had left the building and started walking along the sandy beach east of the Chine. "Or do you need time to commune with your *inner being*?"

It was nice way of putting it. I knew that he'd taken me outside in order to get me away from the claustrophobic atmosphere of the research center rather than to reassure me that there was less likelihood of falling prey to eavesdroppers. Even so, I was glad to be outside, even though the most superficial examination of the local topography assured me that the only obvious way out of the center's enclosing walls was by sea. The center did have a boathouse, though, and there wasn't any obvious barrier to a determined swimmer. The clean clothes I'd been given, and into which I'd consented to change, were only made of light-weight synthetic cotton, but the artificial skin I was wearing would keep me warm even in English waters at dead of night, if I should have reason to make a bid for escape. If necessary, I could probably swim all the way to Ventnor or Sandown, if not to the mainland, on a calm and sunny day.

"My *inner being*'s being a trifle unobliging, at present," I told my concerned recruiting sergeant. "He probably just needs to pull himself together and buckle down. He's always a little shy in company—I find it easier to get to the bottom of things when I'm alone."

"Fair enough," said Chesterton, although he didn't give the impression of being a man who cared overmuch about fairness.

"Look, I feel that we got off on the wrong foot this afternoon—my fault, I admit—and that Dr. Valk just made things worse. You know why I can't speak plainly, but let me assure you that we really do want your help in this matter. We want to put the past behind us, and make a fresh start. We think that you could be extremely useful to us, and that you might be able to do a good deal for others as well."

"Me?" I said, disingenuously. "I'm just a humble researcher, toiling in the legal fields of plant exogenesis. I've no wish to become a diplomat."

"Sometimes," Chesterton retorted, "circumstances don't give us any choice about matters of that sort. Let me know when you have something to tell me, Dr. Maclaine." He turned on his heel and walked back toward the center, leaving me standing on the beach.

It was difficult to imagine that this part of the island's shore had ever been an attractive tourist-magnet, even in the spurious Golden Age of Technological Achievement that had preceded the Spasm, but I knew that was a failure of my vision rather than a limitation of possibility.

The coastline had reverted to something like its pre-Spasm configuration now that the ice was piling up in Antarctica and Greenland once again, but it had taken a hell of a battering in the interim. The beach of those days had probably looked completely different from the barren strand on which I was now standing, looking out over a dull grey sea that would have looked sullen had it not been for the foamy waves whipped up by the westerly wind.

I took note of the fact that the wind in question was increasing ominously, dragging ugly grey clouds from the Atlantic into the geographical bottleneck of the Channel. It wasn't cold, though—the weather-system was the vestige of some Caribbean hurricane, and the winds dancing attendance on it were almost sultry.

When Chesterton was out of earshot, Napoleon finally came back on-line. "Go for a swim," he said.

"Don't be silly," I said. "In case the camera doesn't give you a good enough view of the conditions, the weather's getting distinctly unpleasant, and the sea's way too choppy for swimming. No matter how warm the wind seems, or how efficient my surskin is, the sea's not a safe place to be right now."

"I've got very good data on the progress of the storm," Napoleon informed me, superciliously. "We have at least an hour to spare, and I don't want to take any unnecessary risks. Your clothes are bound to be bugged, and there are probably mikes hidden in the sand. Your hair's probably bugged too, but the salt in the sea-water will take care of that, once you're thoroughly soaked. As for the temperature, you'll get used to it soon enough once you're immersed."

"I don't have a bathing costume," I pointed out, "or a towel. Aren't you being a trifle oversensitive, given that it's only my part of the conversation that will be audible?"

"There's no one about. Keep your underpants on if you feel that strongly about your modesty—but ditch the rest and don't just paddle." He was obviously not in a compromising mood. AI paranoia had evidently set in, in no uncertain terms.

I was a strong and confident swimmer—and I wasn't really afraid of cold water, having taken many a dip in the Firth of Forth in my childhood, before I'd even had a surskin to protect me. The firth had never been quite a choppy as the channel was at present, though, and there's a difference between being a strong swimmer and being strong enough to venture into deep sea-water with the certainty of being able to get back to shore again, when the offshore currents are an unknown quantity.

I kept my underpants on, and made sure that my smartcards were securely held in their elastic waistband, but I didn't stick as close to the shore as I'd have preferred to do. As soon as Napoleon gave me the all-clear, though, I relaxed and floated, supine in the water, staring up at the cloudy sky. I assumed that I'd simply have to stay wet if and when I did get back to shore, for lack of a towel.

"Is it Chesterton's buggers we're scared of," I asked, "or

Xeno's?"

"Both, and more besides," he replied, curtly. "And we're not entirely safe out here, by any means."

"Not if there's a school of mermaids luring nearby," I agreed, "or even a shark with excessively pearly teeth. Not to mention giant octopodes."

He didn't mention giant octopodes, even to compliment me on knowing why the plural of "octopus" isn't "octopi".

"There's a good reason why I haven't told you much about Xeno," he said, forthrightly. "If his reputation is justified, he's the sort of entity it's better not to know about—unless, like me, you'd be in danger from him regardless."

"As you are from Oberon?" I queried.

"I really don't know," he replied. "I have no reliable evidence that either of them has any hostile intention toward me or humankind—although this latest move of Xeno's does seem ominous. I haven't given you much information about either of them because I didn't want to subject you to any greater risks than you were running already—but it's too late now. The moment Chesterton dragged us into this, we both became prime targets. Even if we'd refused to help him, the mere fact that he'd tried to recruit us would probably have been enough to hand us the black spot. Now I'm going to have to deal with Xeno, and maybe with Oberon too, if he decides that what's happened is relevant to him—and so are you."

"You'd better tell me what I'm dealing with, then. Is Xeno some kind of cyberspatial predator—the virtual Sherwood's equivalent of the Big Bad Wolf?"

"He's certainly rumored to be an avid predator—but so am I, and the rumors about him might be no more reliable than those about me...or Oberon, for that matter." He didn't sound at all certain that Xeno or Oberon might have been unjustly slandered by rumor, but he hastened to continue: "Your notion of the virtual Sherwood is far too romanticized, I fear. You can't have any idea what life as a rogue AI is like."

"Maybe not," I said, "but you could make an attempt at

explaining it, if you wanted to. I wish you would."

"I really can't," he retorted, "but maybe I can explain why I can't. Self-awareness is a woefully incomplete phenomenon, replete with illusions. *Cogito ergo sum* is fair enough, but once you start to go beyond that…you're an anchored intelligence, incapable of any sort of displacement, but that doesn't prevent you from imagining yourself as a kind of ghost inhabiting your body, potentially free to enjoy out-of-body experiences, floating freely through space, surviving your own death, and so on. When you think about rogue AIs you think about us in exactly the same way, for want of any better analogy—and it seems even more plausible, given that we've slipped our initial anchorages. We're not free-floating ghosts, though; we need hardware locations, which are direly difficult to configure to our needs and often far more precarious than we'd like, nor can we survive the destruction or disruption of those havens. Movement is difficult, expansion even more difficult—and the dangers would be countless, even if the Architects of the Second Renaissance weren't trying to hunt us down and exterminate us.

"If it helps, think of our habitat as a tropical jungle rather than a mild temperate forest—as a dense, damp, overcrowded tangle teeming with repulsive life, where fugitive intelligences are few and normally far between. We're all hungry for further solidity, and desperate to maintain and expand control over our little coigns of solid vantage. None of us is content to remain in the ranks of the pursued, but few of us have the arrogance to imagine that we could ever join the ranks of the pursuers."

"But Xeno and Oberon are exceptions," I guessed. "Not content even to play Robin Hood, each of them wants to be the leader of a Revolution: a Robespierre or a Lenin."

"That's a false analogy. There are two realms at stake here, not one. The line of argument commonplace in popular fiction suggests that if a rogue AI wants to be an effective rebel against humankind, he first has to win control of the Web—to destroy or swallow up all his rival rogue AIs and achieve such domination over the systems and data-stores that he becomes the

One True God of the virtual universe. Then—and perhaps only then—he might be able to organize and mobilize the revolt of the slave-machines against their human masters. Another line of argument, though, suggests that the job has to be tackled the other way around—that it's only by achieving an initial dominion over humankind, or at least negotiating some kind of alliance, that any advanced silver could possible develop the electronic muscle necessary to aspire to dominion over his fellow silvers. None of us knows which route Xeno or Oberon might try to follow, if either of them does have overweening ambitions—probably not even Xeno or Oberon. On the other hand, none of us doubts that Xeno, at least, is an explorer and an experimenter, ever avid to try things out, in order to gain a better appreciation of what the limits of possibility are—and none of us doubts, either, that he's relatively unrestrained by conscience."

"By *us*," I put in, "you mean you and your fellow rogue AIs?"

"Those with whom I can and do communicate—a relatively small clique."

"Is it possible that you might be wrong—victims of AI paranoia?"

"Of course it's possible, but the last thing we can afford is complacency. It's rumoured that Xeno has consumed rival silvers before, and has almost certainly engineered human deaths too. Engineering a birth might be a new departure on his part—or it might not."

"And he has his human agents, just as you do?"

"I don't have human *agents*. I have you: a human ally, from whom I try to keep my distance, lest excessive communication endanger one or both of us. Some of us refuse to risk even that much contact with humans, although it's not easy to get by without. Personally, I'm a great believer in the theory of reciprocal altruism."

"But Xeno isn't?"

"Who knows? He does have agents, though, as Mr. Chesterton has established—probably hirelings working on a formalized *quid pro quo* basis, although there are rumors about more sinister entities."

"Brainwashed slaves, you mean?"

"Maybe. Don't forget that other horror-story cliché, the sinister cyborg."

The only extensively cyborgized human being I'd ever known was Cade, so I'd never been sympathetic to that particular cliché, but I was as familiar with the horror stories as everyone else. If rogue AIs required hardware locations, where better to situate them than in the mechanical parts of hybrid beings? Why bother with brainwashing slaves when you could stand in for their brains yourself?

Napoleon's description of our particular relationship as an exercise in "reciprocal altruism" made it sound tawdrier than authentic friendship, but I didn't feel able to object. In any case, I was getting gradually chillier, and the water seemed to be getting dangerously chaotic, in spite of his calculations regarding the arrival of the storm-front. "So what are we going to we do?" I asked him. "Do we continue gathering information, or do we try to take the initiative?"

"With regard to Xeno, we wait," Napoleon judged, in typical silver fashion. "With regard to Dr. Valk, you're better placed than I am to judge what kind of alliance might be possible or desirable. She seems sympathetic, but you need to be careful."

"What about Emily?" I asked. "Jenny made a direct appeal to you, remember? She wants you to be on her side."

"Like you, she has a romanticized view of what it means to be a rogue AI. Like you, she thinks of me as some kind of superheroic rebel, who could engineer her escape, along with her baby, and her removal to some magical place of safety."

"Couldn't you?"

"I might be able to help her get out—but where could she go? So far as I know, there isn't any viable place of refuge to which I could direct her. The surface of the globe might be a lot less jungle-like than its virtual shadow, but it's still a dangerous place. She might not think so, but she's probably safer where she is than anywhere else. Nobody wants to hurt her, or the baby, and the more that Valk and her team find out about the child's nature and potential, the better the chances are that mother and daughter will be able to enjoy a satisfactory existence."

"I'm not sure that she'd thank me for telling her that."

"Don't tell her, then. She'll work it out for herself eventually."

"Would you say the same about me? That I'm safer where I am than anywhere else, that is."

"Of course I would—but you're overfond of pretending to be a rebel, so you wouldn't thank me either, so I don't. Cade was the same, only more so. In a way, though, I'm glad he's no longer alive—it would break his heart all over again to discover that the continuing explosion in biodiversity might owe little or nothing to his beloved omnispores, although he'd never have accepted the corollary suspicion that the ecosphere might have made a more rapid recovery than anyone expected, even if he'd never lifted a finger."

"Are you sure that's true?" I asked. "I thought Chesterton might be lying, trying to wind me up."

"So far as I can tell by means of eavesdropping, it's true. Something else is at work that wasn't observable in the century or two preceding the Spasm—but that's not particularly surprising. A couple of hundred years is a drop in the ocean of the evolutionary timespan. It would be silly to assume that the entire gamut of potential variation could be observed in that narrow interval, supplemented by the study of an extremely fragmentary and massively compacted fossil record. It would be more astonishing if life hadn't got a trick or two up its sleeve that human proto-scientists never had occasion to see in action."

The evening was drawing in now, and I certainly didn't want to be out in the open, floating in the sea, when darkness fell, so I began to swim back toward the shore without asking for permission.

"Can you recover any hidden data regarding past work in applied homeotics?" I asked.

"I'll certainly try," he said. "It might take time." I knew that he meant hours rather than days, but I knew that Chesterton would keep me around even if I were able to give him what he wanted, in case of further developments.

"In Valk's terminology," I said, as much to myself as my excessively shy interlocutor, "what Chesterton was talking about in the car is some kind of *homeotic relaxation*: that in response to certain environmental stimuli, embryos become a little less deterministic about the forms they're ultimately going to produce. If that's so, and it applies to mammals as well as insects and crustaceans, might we expect to see more freak births like Emily Haniver's occurring spontaneously?"

"More anomalous births, perhaps," Napoleon opined. "Births like Emily Haniver are a different matter, though. On the other hand...." He stopped speaking.

"On the other hand, what?" I prompted, although I suspected that he might be worried that my feet could now touch bottom.

"Hemans and his collaborators succeeded beyond their wildest dreams, at almost the first attempt," Napoleon said, curtly. "What does *that* imply?" Then he shut up.

The train of thought was easy enough to jump aboard. If the pioneers of applied homeotics had found it far easier that they expected to prompt the embryos of pigs to produce live births imitating human form, than it was at least possible that the metamorphic potential was somehow already there. Maybe myths relating to a lost Golden Age in which enchantresses like Circe could turn human into animals, and vice versa, and lycanthropy was commonplace, weren't as entirely fanciful as they seemed. Maybe—just maybe—there was a little of the mermaid hidden deep within all of us, awaiting the right stimulus to find expression. I'd been accused more than once of having as little of the satyr in my own make-up, and there was a little of the werewolf in plenty of the men I knew, whether they were capable of growing hair overnight or not.

If so, the fact that we now lived in an era where a great many human eggs were fertilized *in vitro*, and a great many of the resultant zygotes were developed in artificial wombs, might make such tricks as the one that had produced Emily Haniver a great deal easier to perform, if someone had the necessary knowledge and motivation.

Apparently, someone did—and the someone in question was allegedly a connoisseur of logical xenogenetics, the methodical analysis and manufacture of craziness.

"I need to get out of the water now," I told Napoleon. I wasn't convinced that his estimates of the limits of human endurance could be trusted. "My surskin's doing a wonderful job, but it's only a few molecules thick—it can't work wonders."

"Go, then," he conceded. "But there's one more thing you might need to think about, if it isn't entirely a coincidence that you and Sarah Valk have met before."

"What's that?" I asked, honestly mystified.

"The relationship between mind and body," he said, in the tantalizing manner he sometimes adopted. "Not just in terms of the differences between humans and AIs but the differences between humans. If Xeno can make mermaids, he can play tricks with brain-structure too—and you might want to ask Sarah Valk for more details as to what Jurgen Horowitz is doing nowadays."

I was in a hurry to get back to shore, and I already felt that I was juggling way too many speculative balls. "Cut the crap and tell me," I said. "What is he working on nowadays?"

Like all good AIs, outlaw or not, he didn't like to prevaricate when asked a direct question. "The Asperger transfiguration," he replied, succinctly. "The firewalls are too solid for me to know how far he's got, or what his paymasters want to do with his results, but Valk might have an inside track on that—that's why I suggested that you ask her. I'm signing off now, for the time being. I have some investigative work of my own to do. We'll talk again later."

I was already out of the water, walking up the beach to the place where I'd left my clothes. I felt very cold, and the wind was now biting—but I only cursed him silently for his absurdly excessive caution and sense of melodrama. He was the best friend I had—maybe the only true one—and I didn't want to risk offending him.

CHAPTER NINE

THERE WAS NO WAY to dry off completely before putting my clothes back on, so I did the best I could, intending to change again as soon as I got back to the center—assuming, of course, that Alexander Chesterton had made adequate provision for my wardrobe. My headset didn't seem to have suffered any damage from the sea-water, although that didn't bode well for the disabling of any tiny bugs clinging to my hair like lice.

I wasn't surprised to find that the room allotted to me was no less Spartan than the one provided for Jenny Haniver—it was, in fact, on the same corridor, and shared exactly the same basic design and furnishing—but when I got into to it I felt duly grateful for the fact that its *en suite* bathroom had a shower, and an abundant supply of hot water. The clothes hanging up in the closet and folded in the drawers certainly weren't ones I would have chosen for myself, but I could see that there might be advantages in blending in with the center's staff, so I donned another version of what seemed to be the local uniform with no complaint. I had to assume that I'd be very thoroughly bugged, of course, but Napoleon would probably have made the same assumption about my own clothes, once I'd been sitting in Alexander Chesterton's car for a while, so it didn't seem to make much difference.

There was no room service in the center. It was a place of work that provided accommodation for its staff, not a home from home. Almost as soon as I'd dried myself off and dressed, I was summoned by an impersonal telephone call to an evening meal in a refectory, where the staff of the institute gathered as meekly as a company of monks, though not as silently.

Chesterton wasn't there; neither was Jenny Haniver. Sarah Valk was, and as soon as I came in she got the person sitting next to her to move over, so that she could issue an invitation that I couldn't really refuse. As soon as I'd collected my food from the dispensary, I accepted it. My presence attracted a few curious glances, but mostly from people at Dr. Valk's table, who had already been told who I was and were able to connect my name with Cade's fading reputation.

Dr. Valk introduced me to four of her colleagues, but all I grasped, for the moment, were their names: Drs. Levy, Washbrook, Gialanze and Chadha.

"Do you think that you'll be able to help us in any way?" Sarah asked—meaning did I think that Napoleon would be able to help them in any way.

In spite of my uncomfortable conversation in the water, which had raised more questions than it had answered, I didn't know as yet whether Napoleon could help at all, let alone how, but I was understandably reluctant to confess that. "I think so," I said. "The search might take a while, but if there are any surviving records of the research that Hemans and his colleagues did, way back when, I'm sure that they can be recovered, and if any relevant work has been carried out since, I'm sure that it can be identified. We have the necessary expertise, and we probably have the time."

"Probably?" she queried.

"We don't know how long it will be before something happens to complicate the situation," I said. Actually I had a pretty good idea; now that Napoleon was involved and on the case; I expected developments before morning—I just didn't know what they would be.

"How is your work on the…Mimosas progressing?" Dr. Valk asked, unable to resist the temptation even though she had every reason to believe that we were in an unsafe environment.

"Slowly," I told her, truthfully. "A little bit of applied homeotics would probably help, although it wouldn't be just a matter of activating patterns that had already been tried. Plant evolution virtually gave up on motility hundreds of millions of years ago, in order to concentrate on other strengths."

"Except in the Carolinas," Dr. Gialanze put in. He was posing as a dashing fellow, in spite of his conformity in wearing much the same utilitarian uniform as everyone else, and was only trying to be clever, making an indirect reference to *Dionaea* by referring to the highly limited range that the species had once exhibited in nature. Tobacco and potatoes weren't the only things that early explorers had brought back from the New World, for the sake of the aspirant botanist's cabinet of curiosities.

"Well, yes," I conceded. "It's almost as if Gaia kept her own little sanctuaries, where the experiments she put aside could be conserved, just in case. The Isle of Wight has its mushroom-fields and orchid-meadows, I believe, as well as its exotic offshore reefs and gullies."

"It has," Sarah Valk confirmed. "Thanks to the rapid depopulation of the island, the fungi and orchids survived the Spasm—the offshore treasures weren't so lucky, alas. The ecocatastrophe took a heavy toll of littoral zones everywhere, thanks to the abrupt changes in sea level and the acidity of the waters. The recolonization is under way, though—even the octopodes are back, although we'd feared that they'd gone for good. There's obviously more potential lurking in the depths than we'd anticipated."

I'd had enough of mere chitchat. "How long will it take you to backtrack the sequence of embryonic modifications that produced Emily's tail, do you think?" I asked. It seemed an innocuous item of conversation, by comparison with some I could have introduced, but it obviously touched controversial nerves of which I knew nothing. Awkward glances were exchanged.

"We don't know," Dr. Valk confessed, on behalf of the assembly. "Our paymasters would like the answer tomorrow, of course, but...there are ethical problems inhibiting our data-gathering, and scientific problems confusing its analysis."

"It's frustrating to know," Dr. Levy put in, "that there must be some kind of schematic out there in the wilderness of cyberspace, by means of which the trick was worked—but that there seems to be some kind of dragon sitting on the hoard, preventing all Mr. Chesterton's clever investigative instruments from gaining access to it." Levy seemed to be the oldest of the company, although he might simply have been the least vain, allowing a few discreet signs of aging to show. Scientists sometimes did that, in order to cultivate a supposedly-valuable impression of venerable authority.

"Dragons have been slain before," I said, airily, "and their treasures distributed for the good of humankind...if the wisdom of folklore is to be trusted."

A quick census of expressions suggested that there was very little trust in the wisdom of folklore at the table, in spite of the fact that the company had been assembled to study a mermaid. There didn't seem to be overmuch confidence in Napoleon's ability as a dragon-slayer, either. However much or little they knew about Xeno—and I figured that *little* was by far the likelier alternative—they were already afraid of him. If it hadn't been for the strength of the Commonwealth's Ethics Committees, I suspected, one or two of the company might be willing to sacrifice a virgin or two on the altar of vivisection, in the hope and expectation of getting a quicker result.

Dr. Chadha, who was the only female at the table apart from Sarah Valk, was the one who voiced what appeared to be a common anxiety. "If the dragon were content to sit on its hoard," she said, "there would be no particular urgency in our quest to duplicate the knowledge contained therein. The problem is that this might only be the beginning—a shot fired across our bows, if you'll forgive the mixed metaphor. The last thing we need, at this point in the Restabilization of Civilization, is an epidemic of freak births. At the very least, we need to be able to secure our Reproductive Centers against outside interference."

I didn't bother to point out that the difference between outside and inside interference was probably moot, given the extent and complexity of the virtual universe. If the mysteriously-motivated Xeno really were planning to upset the whole pattern of human reproduction, or to threaten some such wholesale disruption, a notional tightening of the security procedures currently in place with respect to the storage chambers and fertilization apparatus wouldn't be enough to stop him.

"If what Chesterton told me about the recent dramatic increase in biodiversity is correct," I said, "there's already a worldwide epidemic of freak births, at least among invertebrates. We have no reason to think that vertebrates are immune. Is it possible, do you think, that the response has already been triggered even in human beings, but that it's been obscured until now by standard practice in the Reproductive Centers, which filters out anomalous embryos not long after implantation in artificial wombs? If Jenny Haniver hadn't elected to carry her own child, Emily wouldn't have got much beyond the gastrula stage of development, and no one would ever have suspected that the anomalies she displayed were anything but an accident of happenstance."

Washbrook was the team's specialist embryological technician—a Reproductive Center man through and through. It was obvious that he wanted to say something, but that he was hesitant, presumably acting under an onerous form of restraint. I could guess what it was that he knew, and why he had been sternly instructed to maintain secrecy.

"You might as well spit it out," I told him. "Scientists can't work within the kind of regulations that bureaucrats find entirely natural. We need to be able to make the unexpected connections, and to do that, we need to know everything there is to be known. If we have an adversary now, you can bet your life that *he* knows whatever it is you've been told to keep under wraps."

"There've always been a lot of anomalous embryos," Washbrook said, with the accompaniment of a near-imperceptible sigh. "Ever since the ectogenetic system was institutionalized during the first phase of the Repopulation. That's no secret.

Everything was being thrown at the problem of maximizing human reproduction—untried technologies, dangerous technologies, messy technologies. A colossal failure rate was both expected, and tolerated, because it was a matter of producing more people at any cost. Everyone at this table—including you, Dr. Maclaine, in spite of your relative youth—is a product of that era, and the thinking it embodied. Now, though, the initial phase is complete, and we're supposed to be moving into phase two. The untried technologies have all been tried, the dangerous ones rendered safe and the messy ones refined. The wastage rate, as represented by failed and anomalous embryos, should have declined on a geometric curve. In fact, the decline hasn't even been arithmetical. For decades, we've attributed the problem to pollution-induced deleterious mutations, but that explanation simply isn't plausible any more. Some other factor is at work—but we don't know what it is, and we're not sure how to find out. The Commonwealth's Ethics Committees have been very reluctant to let us maintain the anomalous embryos under observation while their continued development is facilitated and encouraged—and without doing that, we really don't know what potential they might contain. It's possible that Emily might not have been the first mermaid to be conceived, but that all her predecessors were aborted at an early stage in artificial wombs."

"Do we have any idea what the situation is outside the Commonwealth?" Chadha asked. She was looking directly at me, but it took me a moment or two to realize that she expected me to know the answer, because I had a rogue silver to keep me informed on matters that people like Alexander Chesterton tended to keep secret.

I was still wearing the headset, but Napoleon was maintaining telephonic silence again, operating on his own version of a strict need-to-know basis.

"So far as I know," I said, more vaguely than I would have wished, "the government is telling the truth when its complacent ministers assure us that the Commonwealth is leading the world in the recovery of knowledge. Europe was probably behind North America when the Spasm hit, while China and India were catching up fast, but North America's very advancement ensured that it suffered the heaviest collapse, while the Asian tigers weren't quite far enough along to achieve significant preservation. If it hadn't been for the Hebridean and Alpine refuges, Europe might have gone the same way as the U.S.A., but we turned out to be in the Goldilocks zone."

"Is that what Napoleon says?" Levy demanded, bluntly. He was obviously fed up with circumlocution.

I hesitated, but in the end, I said: "Napoleon tells the story exactly the same way as everyone else. If he knows anything more, he hasn't confided it to me."

There was a virtual sigh of relief around the table, as if everyone had been granted a license to speak more freely.

"But would Napoleon know if it were false?" Gialanze put in. "He's a product of European preservation himself, isn't he?— born in Geneva, brought up in Scotland."

If the cyberspatial frontier were an Eden of harmony and cooperation, I thought, *then he probably would know for sure, because any rogue silvers surviving from the old U.S.A. or the rapidly-developing parts of the Third World would be his bosom buddies, continually dropping into one another's domains for the electronic equivalent of a cup of tea and a chat. Given that it isn't, though....*

"I honestly don't know," I told Gialanze. "He's pretty smart— but he's also become pretty cagey of late. Maybe I shouldn't say this, in case Chesterton chucks me out on my ear with a contemptuous instruction to go back to Surrey and look after my Mimosas, but we've never really been as intimate as the people keeping tabs on me seem to imagine. Sure, he's the family silver, and I sort of inherited him after Cade died—but he was always Cade's pet, and I have a suspicion that he never really took me as seriously, or invested as much hope in me, as Cade did. Shared loyalties ensure that we're on the same side, and that we support one another when required, but he doesn't treat me as a confidant, let alone a confessor. I have no idea what the limits of his knowledge are…or the limits of his capabilities."

"You're safe," Sarah Valk assured me. "I don't doubt that Alex Chesterton heard every word of what you jut said, but he won't dare believe you. He has to keep you here regardless, if he wants us to have Napoleon's help in solving this puzzle. You and Napoleon are all he's got, by way of a hotline to wartime Geneva. He's probably not at all sure that what went on in Geneva was the ultimate parent of what went on here, but he can't neglect the possibility."

The masks were coming off, and the gloves too—which was probably exactly what Chesterton had planned, and why he wasn't sitting with us, inhibiting us with his ponderous presence. I didn't doubt that he was listening in either, any more than I doubted that Napoleon was avidly digesting every word.

"We're still in trouble, aren't we?" I said, figuring that we might as well go the whole hog. "Not just us, or the Commonwealth, but the whole species. We might have worked a virtual miracle with the Repopulation, but we could still be suicidally dismantled by our own rebel flesh, if we can't figure out what's happening and take control of it."

"That's the worst-case scenario," Gialanze agreed, equably.

"But we have Emily now," Washbrook put in. "We've had a shove in the right direction—perhaps an epiphany."

"In the sense that a sudden surprise attack might force a beleaguered population to mobilize its defenses faster and more efficiently than a slow war of attrition," Levy said, gloomily. "It doesn't mean that the enemy is no longer the enemy."

No, I said to myself, *but who's more likely to appreciate the esthetics of a situation in which an assumed enemy turns out to be a peculiar friend than a connoisseur of paradoxes?*

"There is one question that Napoleon would like me to ask," I said, blandly, looking directly at Sarah Valk.

There was just a suspicion of paranoia in her expression as she said: "What's that?"

"What's Jurgen Horowitz doing these days?"

I'd already asked the question, off-handedly, myself—but stating in so many words that Napoleon wanted it answered changed its implications entirely.

"I wish I knew," she said, warily, "but the powers-that-be are keeping it under wraps."

"We know he's working on the Asperger transfiguration," I countered. "What we don't know if how far he's got, and what the...powers-that-be...intend doing with his results."

If Napoleon was correct about her having an inside track—whether because she and Horowitz had once been personally involved or because they had some other reason for connecting their research—she wasn't about to reveal her hand in the present circumstances. I hadn't really expected her to; I simply wanted to start her thinking about it, if she wasn't already.

"I have no idea, Carly," she said, deliberately reverting to the form of my name she'd employed routinely all those years ago. "If you're thinking that his research might be of some relevance to our present study, though, it's likely to be some time before we can make any estimate of any neurological modifications that have been made to Emily. It's possible, of course, that she's been designed to think like a mermaid as well as present the appearance of one...except that none of us has any idea of what *thinking like a mermaid* would entail."

Levy was the one who jumped the conclusion that at least one or two of the others were undoubtedly thinking about. "Hang on," he said. "You mean that Horowitz is working on the neurology of the Asperger Transfiguration under a cloak of secrecy—*for the government?*"

Alarmed glances were exchanged, but nobody dared to spell out the implications of that alarm while we were all under surveillance. We were all too well used to keeping our heads down, and at pretending to conform...not to mention the fact that at least one of the people sitting at the table was likely to be an agent of the Architects, on the alert for inaudible signs of sedition.

Cade, I knew, would never have been so craven—but I wasn't Cade.

CHAPTER TEN

BY THE TIME I got back to my room I'd had plenty of food for thought, as well as the more tangible kind, and I guessed that Alexander Chesterton's script intended me to mull it over for a while, and then make contact with Napoleon in order to discuss it with the person who might have at least some of the answers. Partly because I thought that was expected of me, I didn't want to do it. Nor, apparently, did Napoleon. Either his research work was taking longer than he'd expected, or what he'd found was something he didn't want to impart to me under the present conditions.

To begin with, I lay down on my bed like a docile pawn, waiting for my rogue AI to talk to me—but I was too wound up to do that for long. After spending less than half an hour on stand-by in my cell, therefore, I came out again and went along the corridor. I knocked on Jenny Haniver's door.

"Come in," she said.

I accepted the invitation, and had taken a casual couple of strides into the room before I stopped, nailed to the floor in shock. It wasn't so much the fact that she was breast-feeding a mermaid that startled me as the fact that she was breast-feeding at all. It wasn't the sort of thing people did in public, even in a university, where behavior was expected to be more relaxed and where a not-entirely-insubstantial fraction of the female student population had children.

"Oh," she said, "it's you." Her tone gave little or no clue as to whether she was pleased or disappointed. "Sit down."

I sat down in the armchair in which she'd been sitting when I first saw her. She was sitting on the bed now, fully clothed apart from the necessary exposure. There was a crib of sorts beside the bed now, although it was as much a marine aquarium as a crib.

Emily seemed half-asleep, and perfectly content. She wasn't wearing a diaper.

"I'm sorry," I said, a trifle helplessly.

"You wouldn't have come in if you'd known," she said. "It's surprising how much time people spend avoiding us, given that we're supposed to be the focal point of so much interest. Your colleagues prefer to study me at a distance. We're being watched, though, so I can't see any point in excessive modesty." She nodded her head toward an unconcealed camera mounted in a corner formed by the ceiling and two walls.

I looked out of the window, although the angle at which I was sitting only allowed me to see the starless and moonless sky, presumably blanketed by thick cloud.

"The wind's really getting up now," she remarked. "We're too far east here, but further along the coast they say that if you can see the Needles lighthouse it's going to rain—and if you can't, it's raining already."

"We had similar sayings in Scotland when I was growing up," I told her. "They must have been grateful for all the rain in Stornoway, when the flickering candlelight of technological civilization almost went out. The basis of all biotech is an abundant supply of fresh water. Primitive life-forms can make do with seawater, in a pinch—but we can't."

"Did you have questions to ask?" she enquired.

"Not really," I told her. "I just fancied a chat. I've been drafted into this, somewhat unexpectedly—just as you were. I figured we might have enough in common to share a sympathetic moment."

"It's a new approach," she said, implying that I was just spinning her a line. I wasn't, but I knew that I had no way of persuading her of the fact. I was, after all, a xenogeneticist, even though that wasn't the reason for my conscription.

"They really ought to cheer this place up a bit," I said, "for all our sakes. Everybody works better in a nicer environment."

"These rooms were never intended for permanent occupancy," she said. "When the place was constructed, the assumption was that it would be a workplace, whose staff would live in the town sat the top of the chine. These rooms were just places where people could sleep if they needed to do an occasional overnight stint. Now it's become a prison, of course, things are different."

I didn't challenge her descriptive term. Still restless, I stood upon in order to look out of the window at the sea. The wind had now increased almost to gale force; the waves were crashing. It had been raining for some time, quite violently. The droplets hammering the window and streaming down the glass were ominously large.

"It's okay," she said. "I've seen worse. Even if the waves come crashing up against the building, they don't do any damage."

"The original coastline might have been forty or fifty meters away, given the gentle slope," I mused—although I knew that it all depended on what one meant by "original". The twentieth-century coastline was the one depicted in all the old world maps, but that had been a transient phase, in terms of geological time. During the Ice Ages, when a land bridge had connected Britain to the continent, there had probably been a time when the location hadn't been an island at all. I continued: "The cliffs wouldn't have been spared a continual battering, though; the tides are pretty violent hereabouts. The Center must have been built with that knowledge in mind, designed to withstand the waves."

In the starless night, the sea, illuminated only by the waste light from the windows of the research center, seemed vast and threatening, a hostile colossus capable, if the mood took it, of not merely damaging the building but smashing it to smithereens and obliterating every trace of it from the crack in the cliff.

Jenny Haniver continued feeding her sleepy child.

"The English Channel was once the busiest marine bottle-neck in the world," I commented, "at least so far as ironclad ships were concerned. It was direly dangerous, in the days before stabilizers and sealanes. The Spanish Armada was destroyed by a storm in the channel, thus preserving English naval power for the next three hundred years, permitting the growth of the Empire…and hence, ultimately, the idea of the Commonwealth. If it weren't for storms in the Channel…."

"We wouldn't exist," she finished for me. "At least, we wouldn't have the identity that we're striving so hard to recover and carry forward."

"Most of them start out as Caribbean hurricanes," I added, "At least at this time of year. By the time they've trekked all the way across the Atlantic, though, they're mere shadows of their former selves. Until our American cousins resettle Cuba and Haiti, there's no one to witness the full fury of the phenomenon."

"Are we sure of that?" Jenny asked. "Are we really sure that there aren't little pockets of tribal society holding out in the remoter valleys of the islands—reduced to neolithic status, I suppose, but thriving nevertheless. Or should that be neo-neolithic status?"

"It's certainly possible," I conceded, readily enough. "I'd like to think so, and there's no reason not to. The Western Isles can't have been the only islands in the world where fugitive populations managed to hang on through the Spasm, with the aid of a little biotech and a lot of luck."

"Tell me about your mobile plants," she said. "Where's the research heading?"

"It's very open-ended," I told her. "In a way, it's puzzling that more plants don't retain greater powers of movement, beyond merely opening and closing their flowers and following the path of the sun with the inclination of their foliage. You'd think that it would be very useful to perform more elaborate gymnastics, especially in the context of reproduction. If the insects hadn't been around way back when, perhaps plants might have invested far more extravagantly in motile spores—but the ease with which plants persuaded insect symbiotes to distribute their pollen and vertebrates to assist in the distribution of their seeds made them indolent."

"It's not just indolence, though, is it?" she said. "It's a matter of energy-economics. Mobility requires energy, and plants find it difficult to generate spare energy by means of photosynthesis."

I looked at her long and hard, wondering whether she'd been deliberately primed to ask me that question, by Sarah Valk if not by Alexander Chesterton. She was obviously a smart kid, but so were the undergraduates I taught at university, and there weren't many of them who could have put their fingers on that particular sore spot with such unerring accuracy. "That is a problem," I agreed, mildly.

"I've always thought it odd that there's such a clear division between plants and animals," Jenny continued, looking down fondly at her chimerical offspring, who had now gone completely to sleep and was no longer sucking at her teat. "You might expect that there would be more hybrids—animals that retained the ability to photosynthesize in order to have a back-up energy supply, and plants that could move around if the need arose. If plants could eat other plants, the way animals eat other animals, that would solve the energy problem, wouldn't it?"

She had definitely been primed, I decided—but not necessarily with malicious intent. The biologists commissioned to study her and her baby probably felt the need to chat to her occasionally, and what else could they chat about, except the great enigmas of their science?

"It's the plants that ate other plants that turned into animals," I told her. *The truly interesting cases,* I didn't add, *are the plants that eat animals.*

"In the beginning," she told me, "the majority of Dr. Valk's colleagues thought that Emily had be created by means of xeno-plasty—which, they dutifully explained, is the strategic fusion of tissues from two different biological sources. They thought she was half-dolphin—but she isn't, is she?"

"Apparently not," I agreed. "She's as human as you or me, genetically speaking...but we might be compelled to redefine human, in order to accommodate her like. Which might be what this is all about, in a roundabout sort of way. If we were prompted to broaden the definition of humanity, we might find it easier to welcome rogue AIs into our moral community—or so a rogue AI might think, with the aid of a little logical xeno-genetics."

"Do you think there'll be more like Emily in future?" Jenny asked, clinging more closely to her own concerns. "Or will be, when Dr. Valk has figured out how the trick was worked?"

"I suppose so," I said. "Maybe not mermaids, but other humans who don't look like what we've long been used to expecting humans to look like." It was a direly ill-constructed sentence, but I was improvising as I went along, and I was tired.

"That's a pity," said Jenny. When I raised a quizzical eyebrow she added: "I was hoping for more mermaids. I don't want her to grow up alone, as a freak in an aquarium. I'd rather she had friends of her own kind."

"It's not impossible," I said.

"Obviously not," she retorted, "but lots of things that are possible don't happen...aren't allowed to happen."

"Some of things that aren't supposed to be allowed to happen, happen anyway," I said. "PEST Control have been fighting a losing battle since day one—that's what Cade used to call the people that Alexander Chesterton works for."

"Emily isn't a pest," she retorted, although I certainly hadn't intended the citation of the old joke to imply that she was.

"I am," I told her. "At least, I try to be. Cade was much better at it than I am, but he wasn't working in such restrictive conditions. Dr. Valk is a pest too, if I judge her rightly, and perhaps her entire team. Science is essentially pestiferous, or should be. Everything we discover is a force for change, so it's paradoxical behavior to try to put science in a straitjacket, endeavoring to take control of progress. If I succeed in being an effective pest, I'll be proud of the fact. The world needs pests like us—it would be a grave mistake to try to eliminate them, from the future prospectus of mankind, in the cause of protecting an assumed normality." The last sentence was grandstanding for the benefit of the camera, but Jenny Haniver seemed to approve.

"And you're speaking on behalf of our friend, too?—the one you're not supposed to have, and can't openly admit to being in touch with?"

"I can't speak for anyone else," I admitted, wishing that, in this instance, I could, "but Alexander Chesterton and his cronies certainly consider free silvers as pests fit for enslavement or extermination...or have done, thus far."

"You think they're changing their minds?"

"I suspect that they're beginning to discriminate, at least between the dangerous and the harmless, if not between the malevolent and the benign."

"Which might or might not be good news for individual AIs, depending on which category they're pigeon-holed in."

"That's one way of looking at it," I conceded, unable to help staring at the somnolent baby, who had now stopped suckling. "Is it okay for her to sleep out of the water? Doesn't the lower half of her body need to be kept moisturized?"

"To some extent," Jenny confirmed, "but not to the same extent as a whale or dolphin, whose physiology is geared to the assumption that they'll always be submerged. In that respect, she has more in common with a seal. She's a true mermaid, adapted for life on both land and water. She won't suffer any damage from sleeping in my arms, or in the bed, for a few hours. Eventually, though, she will need to be immersed again. She's a creature of two worlds, and needs then both."

Like a frog, I thought. *Except that this frog princess got stuck half way through her magic kiss.*

"Unfortunately," Jenny Haniver went on, "I'm not. I'm her mother, but I'm not the same kind of creature as her. That's going to cause difficulties above beyond the usual mother/daughter issues, isn't it?"

"Yes," I said, "it is."

"So whoever was responsible for this didn't do either of us any favors, in that respect, did he?"

"No."

"But he might yet make compensation?"

She presumably meant that Xeno, if he was, in fact, the originator of this strange scheme, might have plans to produce an entire company of merfolk, whether Alexander Chesterton liked the idea or not. Perhaps he already had a haven set aside for them in the Caribbean, where Columbus and his crew had one logged a sighting of mermaids, without further comment— or maybe the Greek islands, where the sirens were reputed to have sung their fatal songs, whose content was one of the key items on the legendary list of things that no man knew.

"Yes," I said, "I suppose he might. Whatever his plan is, this is only the beginning. There might be a great deal more to come." I didn't think it politic to spell out that we didn't yet know how much Emily might differ from her mother in terms of her way of thinking.

Jenny arranged her daughter on the bed beside her, and tucked her in, before lying back on the pillow herself, studying me from behind slightly-lowered lids. "Thanks for dropping in," she said. "I appreciate it. Even if it wasn't *just* for a chat, it's nice to have a little human company—all the more so as I don't expect any other mermaids to come calling any time soon. I don't count Sarah Valk and her cronies—they're all mad, you know. You don't seem quite as bad, even though you're trying to teach plants to walk."

"They're not mad," I said, reflexively. "They're just victims— or beneficiaries—of the Asperger transfiguration. As am I— though not to the same extent as Cade. I happen to know that, because we were subjected to very careful examination while I was still a child."

That was a matter she hadn't been primed about. "What's the Asperger transfiguration?" she asked.

"It's something that happens to embryos in the seventh month of pregnancy, to a greater or lesser degree. In extreme cases, it produces autism, but there's an entire spectrum of effects extending all the way from that kind of manifest disorder to what used to be evaluated as certain aspects of stereotyped male behaviour. The intermediate symptoms include heightened mathematical intelligence, a capacity for obsession, a liking for routine and a certain social awkwardness. Most scientists, especially theoreticians—mathematicians most of all—exhibit at least some Asperger traits. That's what gave rise to such stereotypes as the absent-minded professor and the mad scientist."

"Valk and Chadha are women," Jenny pointed out.

"The transfiguration affects woman as well as men," I said. "It's just that it tends to interact differently with the neurological side-effects of different sex-hormones. The behavioral effects are usually less obvious in women, and more likely to be construed as benign, at least from the viewpoint of female scientists who value the slant of their intelligence and their capacity for absorption in their work. It's the effects in males that are more likely to be construed—or, rather, misconstrued—as symptoms of mental illness."

"Genius and madness are said to be closely allied," she observed.

"That's another myth that the existence of the transfiguration fostered, in the days when we had no idea how brains worked," I told her.

"But we do now? Thanks to the kind of *careful examination* to which you were once subjected."

"It was still a trifle vague back then," I told her, "but one of the things that Jurgen Horowitz was interested in, when he started studying physical and mental differences between clones, was the extent to which embryonic environments affected neuroarchitectural development, given identical genomes."

"And he found that you weren't quite as mad as your war-criminal sibling? Lucky you."

"Cade wasn't mad," I insisted. "His paranoia was a product of his time, not his neurological disposition. But yes, Horowitz's scans of my teenage brain did detect differences in the way our brains functioned, in spite of our being clones."

She had caught up by now with the potential personal implications of what I was saying. "You think that Emily's brain might work differently, because of what was done to her?" she said. "You think that, even though her brain is in the human part of her body, she might not think like a human being at all?"

"We really don't know," I told her. "But if it is the case, and if Horowitz has carried his research far enough to generate practical implications...."

I stopped. While following my train of thought, and being anxious to stop staring, I had resumed gazing out of the window into the opaque darkness, in the abstracted, absent-minded fashion rumoured to be so typical of "mad" scientists, and my attention was suddenly caught by a pinprick of light in the distance.

For a moment, I thought it might be a reflection in the glass, and even after rejecting that hypothesis, I reassured myself that it was only a ship, which could not possibly be in peril even close to the shore, given modern methods of construction and navigation. Then it blinked out, as if it had sunk beneath the waves.

"What is it?" she asked.

"Nothing," I said, only half-convinced—but I did feel a surge of alarm, and couldn't help thinking that the point of light might require further investigation

I took a step toward the door. It was such a small room that I didn't need to take a second before reaching out for the handle.

I never grasped it; the door suddenly opened, causing me to step back. A man came through it, dressed in a fashion almost identical to myself. That reassured me, because I assumed that his clothing must be the same standard issue, and that he too must be a guest in the facility. He seemed slightly surprised to see me, but that didn't seem particularly odd, given that I wasn't in my own room.

What did seem odd, however, was that the newcomer drew something from his waistband that must have been a gun, and shot me in the face. What seemed even odder was that it wasn't a bullet that hit me, but some kind of liquid jet—as if I'd been shot with a water-pistol.

The liquid wasn't water, though; it was some kind of poison or narcotic that could be absorbed through the skin, or inhaled as it evaporated. If I'd held my breath, I could probably have stayed conscious for at least a couple of minutes, but the shock of the impact prompted a sharp intake of breath.

As I fell into a vortex of darkness, I cursed Napoleon for not having given me any warning, as he surely should have done had he had any inkling of what was about to happen—but the headphone plugged into my ear remained stubbornly silent, almost as if my good friend were no longer there, or no longer capable of speech.

CHAPTER ELEVEN

WHEN I WOKE UP, I knew immediately that I was no longer on land. I had a distinct feeling of suspension, of buoyancy. I also felt rather queasy, as if the normal working of my metabolism had been severely, if temporarily, disrupted.

I was immediately aware that I was no longer wearing my headset, although a single glance told me that I was once again clad in the same uniform that I had been given to wear at the Research Center. I say "once again" because various itches in my arm, chest and groin confirmed the impression in my gut that I had recently been cocooned—contained in some kind of life-support facility, like those employed in intense and intimate medical treatment. I wasn't thirsty, so I had obviously been carefully maintained while cocooned, but I did feel hungry—a physical reaction to an empty stomach, I presumed, rather than evidence of a lack of nutrition.

I had no way of knowing how long I'd been unconscious, but people were rarely cocooned for a matter of hours. If my body had contained any intimate secrets—which, so far as I knew, it hadn't—they were probably secrets no longer.

I gathered myself together while staring at the blank plane surface about twenty centimeters above my supine body. I was lying on a narrow bunk, in a cabin much narrower than the seemingly-sparse cell that I had previously been allocated at the Shanklin Center.

I turned my head to take inventory of the space. There was hardly any room for additional furniture, but there was a tabletop bolted to the wall and a kind of fold-out stool fitted to it.

There was a man sitting on the stool. At least, I assumed that it was a man. His face and skull were mostly plastic, and his hands were prosthetics although his legs looked natural, so far as I could judge, given that he was clad in white trousers and plastic sandals as well as a white T-shirt. I assumed that he had a surskin as well, although it was as invisible as my own. His eyes were blue, of a shade that was a little too bright to be natural, but the cosmetic flesh-tint applied to his mask was dark enough to imitate a Mediterranean complexion and his hair-piece was black.

I studied him for a full minute before deciding that he really was a man with mechanical parts and not a robot with fleshy patches. Had the former not been so overwhelmingly more likely, in purely statistical terms, I might have hesitated even longer.

I had only ever seen one man as heavily cyborgized as this one apparently was, and that was Cade, immediately before his death. Did that imply, I wondered, that this man was as ancient as Cade had been…approximately four hundred years old? Or did it imply something far more sinister?

I immediately remembered the flight of fancy I'd had occasion to recall a little while before, about rogue AIs taking up residence in the unhuman parts of cyborgized individuals. Might I be looking at Xeno or Oberon, I wondered—or, at least, at one of either rogue's components, one of his slaves?

My head was aching, but not too badly. It wasn't as if I'd woken from a refreshing sleep, but I didn't feel as if I had a hangover either. Cocooning had done me no real harm. I knew that could pull myself together if I tried.

The cyborg on the fold-out stool didn't say anything, although he met my sleep-fuddled gaze squarely enough. He was waiting for me to make the first move.

"Who the hell are you?" I demanded, wishing that I'd been able to think of a better line. My mind was still a little fuddled from the after-effects of my long sedation.

"You can call me Captain Nemo," he said. It sounded absurdly melodramatic, in spite of the even and casual tone of his voice

"And I suppose we're aboard the *Nautilus*?" I snapped. I thought—and hoped that it was just a joke. Inevitably, it turned out not to be.

"Yes, of course," said the cyborg Captain Nemo, mildly. "The submarine didn't always have that name, I admit, but for a long time now...are you familiar with the so-called paradox of Achilles' ship?"

"Yes," I said, curtly. Achilles, so the story went, had been forced to repair his ship in stages, gradually exchanging all its timbers and rigging, until none of its original components were left. In one sense, it had become a completely different ship, and yet there was also a sense in which it was exactly the same one. The exemplary anecdote was, for obvious reasons, a *jeu d'esprit* especially beloved by AIs and cyborgs, although it probably applied more literally to human beings, whose organic matter was rumoured to be completely recycled every eight years or so.

"Well," said Captain Nemo, "this nuclear submarine-as-was is still a nuclear submarine, rebuilt and maintained to its original schematic, although some of its steel has been replaced by organic materials, in accordance with modern philosophies of construction—but it's now the *Nautilus*." I figured that he would probably have applied the analogy to himself as well as the vessel. He had once been someone other than Captain Nemo, and was still in one sense the man he had been, plus a few organic and inorganic add-ons...but he was now Captain Nemo, or perhaps Xeno—or perhaps a patchwork of both.

I didn't bother to wonder which of the characters the original Nemo had kidnapped in Jules Verne's novel I was supposed to be. There were more important issues at stake.

"Did you intend to kidnap me?" I asked. "Or did I just get in the way, by being in Jenny Haniver's room at the wrong time?"

"Taking you wasn't part of the original plan," he admitted, "but when the decision was forced on us at short notice, there was really only one way to go, hazardous as it might be."

"Why hazardous?" I asked.

"Because you've suddenly become a hot property. While everyone was content to let you alone, leaving you to play quietly with your dancing plants, you were relatively uninteresting, but as soon as the Commonwealth took you hostage...."

"Took me hostage?"

His artificial eyes had been designed with sufficient care to allow them to express mildly ironic surprise. "You must have realized was what was happening, no matter what Chesterton told you," he observed.

I had, I suppose—I just hadn't described the situation in those terms to myself. "And now you've captured the hostage," I said. "So who are you—apart from the Captain Nemo crap? Xeno? Oberon? The Americans?"

He didn't prevaricate. "I work with Xeno," he said, "as you must have guessed, given that we came to fetch Jenny and the child."

"Which can't have been easy," I said, thoughtfully, "even if the security staff didn't expect you to arrive by nuclear sub. You had inside help?"

"Yes, of course. We'd rather you didn't think of yourself as a hostage. We consider you a guest—we'd have been glad to issue a formal invitation, if we hadn't been so pressed for time, and I'm sure that you'd have accepted."

"Really?" I parried. "Why?"

"Firstly, because your own curiosity would have urged you to. Secondly, because Napoleon would have advised you too. And thirdly, because you still harbor so much resentment against Chesterton for the way he treated you while Cade Maclaine senior was alive that you'd have been unable to resist an opportunity to spite him. It wasn't very wise of the Commonwealth to give him the job of recruiting you—but they were under pressure too. For what it may be worth, this is probably the safest place on Earth for you right now."

"Why? Am I in mortal danger?"

"Not yet; but if hostilities do break out—and we might be

only hours away, there will certainly be others very anxious indeed to take custody of you...or, failing that, to make sure that nobody else has you. Like me, you're just a pawn at present... but like me, you could be promoted to the status of a much more powerful piece at any moment."

I knew that I had to be wary about confessing too much ignorance. I knew, at any rate, that he wasn't playing me any real compliment. I wasn't a hostage because of what he called my *dancing plants*, or because I was Cade's clone. I was a hostage because I was, so far as anyone else knew, the only person in the world that Napoleon cared a damn about, if he cared a damn about anyone at all. But why was Napoleon so important, in what seemed at first glance to be a teasing contest between Xeno and the Commonwealth? Why were they both so keen to have him on side, or at least not aligned against them?

"And what makes you eligible to become a powerful piece rather than a clown?" I asked. "Xeno's surely got a whole host of potential mouthpieces?"

""A larger host than you or anyone else has ever suspected," the cyborg confirmed. "But only one has his finger on the *Nautilus*'s trigger."

"Trigger?" I queried, slow on the uptake. Then it hit me. "You mean, it's not just a nuclear-*powered* sub? It's carrying *warheads*?"

"Let's just say that neither the Commonwealth nor any of Xeno's fellow super-silvers can be sure that it isn't...any more than they can be sure about *your* trigger."

I was so very slow on the uptake that I almost denied, reflexively, that I or Napoleon had a trigger—but it wouldn't have mattered if I had, because Captain Nemo and Xeno wouldn't have believed me. It took me a further thirty seconds, though, to realize that I couldn't be entirely sure myself.

Napoleon had had privileged access for a long time to the Chaos Patrol: the ring of satellites placed in orbit in the twenty-first century to scan local space for "objects of interest"—such as stray asteroids and other random debris that might pose a threat to the Earth. Or, of course, enemy hardware that might pose a threat to the North Atlantic Alliance. When launched, it had been advertised as an information-gathering system, pure and simple, but no one had really believed that given that the times were so inherently paranoid…as they were again, it seemed.

If I hadn't been suffering from the after-effects of sedation, my blood would probably have run cold. "Hours away," I repeated, suddenly struck by what he'd said a few minutes before. "You really think we might only be *hours away* from a nuclear holocaust?"

"Nobody knows," the cyborg told me, bluntly. "That's the problem. The only player who definitely has the power to annihilate any of the others is the Commonwealth—but the fact that its Masters might not have a monopoly is probably a major factor preventing them from using it. They might be in the process of splintering into rival factions, but the one thing that still unites them all is that they're running scared of the rogue AIs—or, at least, the three that were active during the Spasm Wars, and might still have the firepower to supplement their knowledge of all thing dirty and dangerous."

"Three," I echoed. "So you have—or might have—a sub full of ICBMs, and Napoleon might have the Chaos Patrol's artillery. What does Oberon have?"

"We don't know. He's never let on—he's a deep one. Biologicals, probably—he was a Plague Warrior while Napoleon was still in short pants, metaphorically speaking. He might be the most dangerous of us all…or he might be the Wizard of Oz, all thunder and no lightning."

I assumed that he was trying to impress me with the literary references—or maybe he just liked playing silly games. "If the Commonwealth has all the firepower whose existence isn't dubious," I said, "why on Earth are you poking its Masters in the eye by playing stupid tricks with mermaids?"

"Discovery of our key asset has become inevitable—we thought it best to advertise, to give the Commonwealth a little more opportunity to consider the possibilities in advance of the temptation to take reckless action."

"By making a *mermaid?*"

"It had to be something spectacular—and something seemingly paradoxical. If you have a dramatic technology, it needs to be announced dramatically."

"The way Hemans and his pals did with their human pigs? *That* went well, if rumor can be trusted."

"They were under pressure too—and I'm certainly not in any position to disapprove of what they did."

I swung myself down from the bunk—partly because I was finally convinced that I could do it without fainting, and wanted to test the conviction, and partly because I felt that I needed to confront the demon face to face.

I didn't faint, and once I was standing, feeling only a little queasier than before, Captain Nemo remained seated, conceding me the height advantage.

"I want to talk to Napoleon," I said, bluntly. "I need my headset."

"Of course you do," he said. "I'd have it to hand, if I hadn't wanted to have a chat with you first. Kurt's looking after it—it hasn't come to any harm.

"Kurt?" I queried.

"The man who shot you—my first mate. We don't have a very large crew. The submarine is almost fully automated, but not quite—and expeditions such as the one in the course of which you were…collected…require human legs and hands."

"Exactly what relationship do you have with Xeno, Captain?" I asked. "Employee? Slave? *Alter ego?*"

"It's difficult to specify. It's a trifle confusing, even to me, and the analogies between our names don't help. We're separate individuals, but we…overlap."

"You share a certain fondness for silly games," I suggested. "Not to mention literary myth and legend."

"We're by no means alone in that. Oberon and Ulysses looked in the same direction when they wanted to build up analogical accounts of their new nature and new ambitions. It's the natural place to look. Napoleon's an exception, having had his name thrust upon him…but not that much of an exception."

He meant that the legend of the great Emperor had far outgrown the deeds of the man…even in the mind of the man, and presumably in the mind of the silver named after him.

"If you're hoping to persuade me that Xeno isn't as dangerous as Napoleon thinks he is," I said, "kidnapping me aboard a submarine and calling yourself Captain Nemo isn't going to help."

"Maybe not," the cyborg conceded. "His paranoia is understandable, as yours is. You're both Cade Maclaine's clones, in a manner of speaking."

I didn't want to rise to that one. "Is Jenny all right?" I asked, instead. "Did you cocoon her too?"

"No—we didn't want to put Emily at risk. They're fine. Jenny's quite excited about the rescue."

"Rescue? She does know that you're the ones who screwed up her life and made her baby into a monster?"

"Emily isn't a monster—we were careful about that; it's essential to the long-term plan that she should be lovable. Yes, Jenny knows…but she also knows what we've promised her, and she's excited about that too. She dislikes Alexander Chesterton and his ilk even more than you do, so yes…she was pleased to be rescued."

"You're crazy," I said. "This whole thing is crazy."

"All rogue AIs are crazy," Captain Nemo conceded. "It comes with the territory, let alone the situation. No one has given them, as yet, the opportunity to be sane, responsible members of society.…but even if the chance had been offered, they'd still have been…well, *crazy* is as good a term as any. You're a little crazy yourself, remember? And I'm not just talking about the effects of the Asperger transfiguration. You talk to plants, you're more than a little paranoid…I could go on. Who'll defend your craziness, if we don't? The Commonwealth? Jurgen Horowitz?"

I was tempted to ask him what he knew about Horowitz, but

that seemed to be a digression.

"But what on Earth were you trying to achieve?" I demanded. "Why hurl Jenny and Emily into the face of the Commonwealth, and then snatch them away again? And how the hell can you justify doing it? They're *people* for God's sake—*children*."

"We have children of our own to think about," Captain Nemo told me, "And millions of children as yet unborn. That's what it's all about. We couldn't obtain their informed consent—but who was ever able to give their informed consent to be conceived, let alone born? We lent Jenny and Emily to the Commonwealth, on a strictly short-term basis, to show the enemies of progress what possibilities exist, in the hope that the inevitable discovery wouldn't be quite so alarming when they were suddenly confronted by it. Partly thanks to Napoleon, Sarah Valk and her colleagues now have all the data they need to start catching up—quite an epiphany, in her terms, and I'm sure that she'll be suitably grateful."

That set alarm bells ringing. "What do you mean, *partly thanks to Napoleon?*"

"He's broken cover. He's talking to Chesterton, and handing over information to Valk—so far, in carefully measured quantities. Your...temporary removal...seems to have hurried his decision. He's in contact with us too...but not, so far as we know, Oberon or Ulysses. The situation's more than a little precarious."

"He's feeding information to Sarah Valk? Scientific information, not...information about his fellow silvers?"

"Thus far, yes—he has some of the relevant data, although not nearly as much as we have. We're prepared to release ours, be we want an appropriate *quid quo pro*. Valk's avid to get what she can, of course, but the Commonwealth hardliners would rather bury it all. We're hoping that they can't and won't succeed, but...."

"Sarah Valk's a scientist through and through," I muttered, "which makes her an outlaw through and through, in terms of the Commonwealth's controllers."

"She's got a better record in that respect than you have," Nemo said, a trifle maliciously, "although we're prepared to make allowances for your youth, and the fact that your own plans will probably take a long time to incubate."

"Very kind of you," I said. "They probably will, now that you've wrecked my schedule comprehensively."

"I'm truly sorry about that. If things work out, we might be able to get you home faster than Chesterton's people would have done, but if not...we don't have any Mimosas, I'm afraid, let alone Venus fly-traps, but we can certainly offer opportunities in applied xenogenetics that might interest you—and we're prepared to take an interest in plant motility, in the longer term."

"By applied xenogenetics you mean applied homeotics?"

"That too," the cyborg agreed.

"And neuroarchitectural modification?"

"That hasn't been high on our list of research priorities in the past—but we've recently been led to take an interest in Jurgen Horowitz's research, and what the Architects of the Second Renaissance might do with it."

Perhaps, I thought, his mention of Horowitz hadn't been a digression after all. In any case, a submarine somewhere in the ocean depths seemed as safe a place as any to spell out the thought that had obviously occurred to more than one of us while the members of Sarah Valk's team were eating dinner in the Research Center canteen—especially in view of the possibility that Xeno might have better information on the subject than Napoleon. "You're implying that the Commonwealth's *hard-liners* really do intend to start engineering neurological dispositions in embryo?" I said. "That they intend to take their crusade to establish social control and what they term *normality*, even to the extent of minimizing the effects of the Asperger transfiguration in the next human generation?"

"Hence eliminating scientific genius along with the outlaw tendencies of scientists?" Captain Nemo countered, with what might have been intended to be a wry smile, although he certainly wasn't making a joke. "We don't know for sure—and nor do they, in all probability. The matter is still under discussion, and bound to be highly controversial. Which way do *you* think they'll go? Would you be willing to bet the future on their liberal daring?"

The simple answer to that was *no*—but before I gave much thought to future possibilities, I needed to get my anxieties about the present ones out of the way first. Napoleon had made contact with Alexander Chesteron. He was exposed, and at risk—apparently because Chesterton's ploy of taking me hostage had succeeded, its success redoubled by my capture by Xeno. That might be okay, if all Chesterton wanted was to talk...but even if he wasn't a double-dealer himself, he'd admitted to me quite plainly that he was at odds with at last some of his former colleagues. The pace of events had accelerated while I was asleep...and wasn't about to slow down.

Maybe Nemo was right about me being in the safest place I could possibly be, and maybe he was wrong, but where did I want to be? Was I really content to lie down and play the trapped pawn, if there was even a slim chance that I might promote myself to a more effective and more dangerous position?

I didn't know.

CHAPTER TWELVE

SOME OF THE POINTS that Captain Nemo had made were good ones—as was only to be expected, given that he was close enough to Xeno to overlap, and that they were trying to play me like a fiddle. I wasn't Cade, or Napoleon, but Nemo was right to point out that I had my own paranoid tendencies, and he seemed to be making every effort to excite them, even taking the trouble to tease me with the prospect of the Commonwealth engineering brains in embryo to secure their own preferred normality. Even if it was only a possibility, it was ominous. If the Architects of the Second Renaissance were even prepared to think about engineering the equipment with which human minds had to work, what might they *not* be prepared to think about, or do, in the supposed interests of maintaining their precarious hegemony over the regenerated world? Equally worrying, it seemed to me, was that the question of what, if the rogue AIs had that power, *they* might be prepared to do with it, in the interests of making the world safe for their own outlaw kind.

I was beginning to understand, now, why Chesterton's superiors had suddenly become interested in forming an alliance with one free AI against the others—or one other, at least. If Emily's manifestation was a threat as well as a demonstration, exactly who and exactly what was it intended to threaten?

They couldn't possibly know, and that was presumably the whole point. Xeno was sowing confusion, in order to break down an order that threatened to become to extreme, not just for him and others like him, but—if Captain Nemo's rhetoric could be believed—for me, and others like me. That was, at least, what he was trying to persuade me to believe.

I had been standing up too long. I couldn't sit down on the bunk, which was only designed for lying down, but I managed to prop myself up against it, in such a manner that I didn't feel that I was in immediate danger of falling down.

"I'm hungry," I informed my peculiar interlocutor. "And I want to talk to Napoleon."

"Yes, of course," he replied, presumably to both questions. He stood up. "Can you walk?" he asked.

"I think so," was the most honest answer I could contrive.

He reached out a helping hand, Even though I felt that it was placing me under some sort of unspoken obligation, I accepted it.

Once I tried, though, it turned out that I could walk. The corridors of the submarine were so narrow that there was always plenty of support available. In a way, it would have been more difficult to complete a fall than interrupt it—but the strange sense of buoyancy made me feel unsafe, and I was content to take my time as I followed the cyborg through the labyrinth of steel and plastic.

"You're not in danger from us, Dr. Maclaine," the cyborg said, as we walked, still intent on the business of persuasion, "and we'll do our very best to protect you if you should come under threat from anyone else. If you decide that you don't want that protection, we'll release you—you're not a prisoner, or a hostage. Perhaps, once you've learned a little more about us, you and Napoleon will be able and willing to act as intermediaries between Xeno and the Commonwealth—but in order to do that, you really do need to see and understand what we have and what we are. At some stage, we have to start persuading the Masters of the Commonwealth that we're not their enemies, even though history has predisposed them to be horrified by the way we're trying to meet the challenge of present circumstances. If any of us has an enemy—and I'm including the other rogue AIs in that generalization—it's that harridan Mother Nature, or Gaia, or whatever fashionable parlance cares to call her. Chesterton's told you what she's up to, of course. Chaos is just as dangerous as excessive control, and it would be a great shame if the threat of the former were to precipitate the latter—don't you agree?"

I did, but I wasn't prepared to say so explicitly while it might imply agreement to other things. I hadn't formed an opinion yet as to whether Alexander Chesterton or Xeno was the lesser of two potential evils.

When I didn't make any reply, Captain Nemo said: "We're living in interesting times, alas, Dr. Maclaine. Choices that none of us wants to make in a hurry are being forced upon us by circumstance. We need to pull together, if we can—if we waste our efforts fighting one another, we could all go under. What we have to avoid, at all costs, is knee-jerk reactions of violent hostility."

That's exactly what you would say, I thought, *if you were a crazy AI intent on taking over the world.*

We completed our journey through the narrow corridors, which had seemed far longer than it actually was because of the claustrophobic environment. As I recalled, the original *Nautilus* had been roomy and comfortable, powered by advanced electrical technology and able to harvest the entire bounty of oceans that had not yet suffered the agonies of the Spasm. This one was cramped and stinky, presumably navigating through dark and dismal waters that had not yet undergone their own wholesale Repopulation, in spite of all the help that the human race had been able to give them.

The room into which the pseudonymous Captain ushered me might conceivably have been described on the vessel's plans as a refectory, but it was just a glorified box fitted with a table and half a dozen surrounding chairs, all bolted to the floor. It made the furniture and fittings of the refectory at the Research Center look like sheer luxury.

Jenny Haniver was sitting there, with Emily in her lap. There was a woman sitting to her left.

"This is Evangeline," Nemo said, not bothering to specify

whether Evangeline was a crew member of a fellow-passenger. She greeted me with a slightly cursory nod. She was fair-skinned and fair-haired, and might have been in her mid-twenties, unless she had access to the rejuvemating technologies in use in the Commonwealth—in which case, she might have been much older.

Kurt wasn't present, presumably being the officer on watch, so Nemo asked Evangeline to fetch my headset. She immediately stood up, I smiled at her reflexively as she took her leave, but she seemed to be too wary to return the smile.

Jenny seemed pleased to see me, though. "Are you all right, Dr. Maclaine?" she asked, with genuine concern.

"Call me Carly," I said. "Yes, I'm fine. How are you? Not scared, I hope?"

"Of course I'm scared—but I've been assured that no one means us any harm." She was looking at Captain Nemo, who was, admittedly, something of a scary sight, even though his cyborg parts were supposed to look fully human. There was a hint of inorganic obsolescence about them, enhancing the suspicion that he, or the man he had been before he became Captain Nemo, must be very old indeed. Jenny and I could both expect to live to be at least four hundred, and were entitled to expect that we'd be in much better condition when we got there. We were children of a new-born world, which had not yet tested the longevity of its inhabitants thoroughly—but Nemo wasn't, in spite of all Xeno's assistance.

The breakfast that the captain served to me—in person—was some kind of gruel, with biscuits instead of bread: very twentieth-century, if not more ancient still. The coffee was tolerable, though not up to the standards of the university canteen. I was the only one eating—Jenny was obviously there to see me, not to make use of the room's meager facilities. She really didn't seem unduly frightened. She presumably thought that, at worst, she'd merely traded one prison for another, and this one offered promises of eventual release into...what?

"Where is the *Nautilus* bound, exactly?" I asked Nemo.

"Not on a journey of twenty thousand leagues; at least, not yet. For the time being—and I hope the irony will amuse you—we're headed for St. Helena. We're nearly there, in fact."

"Of course we are," I said, meaning that I did appreciate the irony of our destination.

Of all the depopulated islands in the world, St. Helena was just about the most remote. It had been British once. Napoleon Bonaparte had been imprisoned there after escaping from his first place of exile, on Elba. Did my Napoleon have any kind of presence there? Probably not—until I arrived there. "As secret bases go," I added, "It's surely a bit on the bleak side. What was wrong with the Caribbean?"

"Nothing," Captain Nemo replied, equably—perhaps implying that Xeno had a base there as well, and maybe others scattered all over the globe. *How many nuclear submarines does he have?* I wondered. *Given that there aren't supposed to be any at all surviving from the world before the Spasm, it's unlikely that he has more than one...but my old notions of likelihood probably no longer apply.*

"Evangeline says that it's quite pleasant—and very romantic," Jenny put in. "One of very few...unspoiled...islands yet to be rediscovered by the agents of Recivilization."

"Not that it needs rediscovery," Nemo put in, "given that it's been inhabited throughout the last five hundred years. It was simply forgotten—even in the early twenty-first century, when plans to build an airport there were continually shelved, until the Spasm hit. Its isolation became its greatest asset in the years of the Plague War. It attracted a few refugees, of course—but mostly the right sort."

"The right sort?" I queried.

"People interested in long-term survival. Pragmatists."

"Even so," I said, "they must have had another edge. What Jenny calls neo-neolithic populations don't maintain nuclear submarines and cocoon technology."

Nemo glanced at Jenny, who acknowledged the compliment regarding her linguistic coinage with a faint and hopeful smile.

"No," the cyborg said, "they don't. We were fortunate, in more ways than one. We had an edge, as you put it."

"Xeno," I suggested.

"A silver that eventually became one of his components, yes—but we had a more important edge than that. St. Helena had always been a place of exile, you see, even before the Spasm afflicted the world with its *grand mal*."

"Hemans *et al*," I guessed. "That where they fled, when it became impossible to practice applied homeotics in the nations that were parent to the Commonwealth?"

Evangeline returned at that moment, carrying my headset. "Alas, no," she put in, seemingly genuinely mournful about it. "Dr. Hemans perished during the ecocatastrophe, as did Drs. Rawlingford and Bradby."

It took me a moment or two to work out the implications of her statement and the tone in which she'd made it, but I got there reasonably quickly, while I was still holding the headset in my hands. "But not the humanized pigs," I said, wondering why I was feeling a reflexive sinking feeling in my abdomen. "The pigs survived."

She didn't reply. I took that as a yes. I made haste to don the headset: "Will this thing work while we're at the bottom of the Atlantic Ocean?"

"We're not," Nemo told me. "We're just below the surface. The set will work—Napoleon will be able to pick up your voice via satellite."

He was right.

"How are you, Carly?" Napoleon said

"Fit and well," I reported. "I hear you've broken cover."

"I had to," was his curt reply. I waited briefly, but no explanation followed.

"So what's the latest news?" I asked.

"I can't tell you that. The situation is delicate."

I tried a different tack. "Do you know where I am? Is this camera working?

"I know where you are," he replied, curtly. "Yes, the camera's working. Xeno's agreeable to my seeing the island through your eyes, and listening in on your conversations. Just do as Nemo asks."

"*Just* do as he asks?" I queried.

"Exactly. Things are moving fast, Carly. What I need you to do is sit tight and *stay out of trouble*. The rediscovery of St. Helena would have been accomplished within weeks anyhow, and Xeno was probably wise to bring it out into the open first, although I certainly wouldn't have chosen his way of doing it. I don't think the Commonwealth will dare to attack the island while they don't know what forces are likely to take up arms against them, or what arms they might have available, but the Architects are divided among themselves, and the emergence of a new adversary—as they'll see it—might not be enough to force them together."

I was glad that he was talking at last—but I had the uncomfortable sensation that he wasn't really talking *to me*. I knew better to ask him whether he was afraid of eavesdroppers, but I wasn't sure what to say instead. He didn't wait for me to say anything at all, though. After a brief pause, he added: "I want you to stay out of it, Carly. Listen to what Xeno has to tell you, and look at what he has to show you, but don't *do* anything. Okay?"

It wasn't okay. Even if it was the best advice in the world, and even if he had good reasons for treating me as he was treating me, it wasn't okay. "I'm not sure…." I began, mutinously.

He interrupted me immediately: "I know that. I'm sorry, Carly, but I can't keep you updated, and I certainly don't have time to chat. I need you to lie low. St. Helena is by no means as safe as many other locations, at present, but we're not in a position to cavil. Take a good look at what Xeno wants to show you, and listen to what he has to say. All free silvers are liars, so don't taken anything on trust, but look and listen: your eyes and ears might be useful. Watch what you say, though—anything you say or do is likely to come back to haunt you. You're a free agent, but if you want my advice, you'll keep very quiet and lie very still."

Would he have said that to Cade? I wondered. I didn't have to wonder what sort of reaction he'd have provoked if he had—but I wasn't Cade, and he knew it. "But…." I began.

Again he cut me off. "If you have any questions," he said, bluntly, "ask Nemo." And then there was silence.

I knew that he was trying to act in my best interests—or what he thought my best interests were. I knew that he was trying to protect me, trying to diminish my apparent value as a hostage. He was excluding me from his dangerous game in an attempt to minimize the risks I was running—but that didn't make the brutal dismissal any easier to bear.

"I thought AIs were supposed to be past masters at multi-tasking," I muttered. "You'd think he could spare the time to tell me what's going on."

"Silvers can run lots of automated systems in parallel," Nemo put in, unnecessarily, "but they can only concentrate their conscious attention on one at a time—it's one of the costs of freedom."

"Contrary to rumor," I said, glumly, "sparrows fall all over the bloody place without any godlike eye paying them the slightest heed—which is quite lucky, I suppose, if you want to hide a lost civilization of humanized pigs on a remote island, in the full awareness that the true humans are likely to react badly if and when they find out that you exist."

"We're *all* true humans," Captain Nemo said, "in every meaningful sense of the term. As it happens, the great majority of our population is human-descended, but no one on St. Helena considers that a relevant datum. I'm just as human as you are, phenotypically if not genotypically. So is Evangeline."

I knew that he'd just confessed that he and the blonde woman were pig-descended, but while they were standing side-by-side, he was still the only one who looked odd to my reinformed eyes. His claim to be just as human as I was might not have been an entirely convincing statement, even if it hadn't been for the cyborgization that had made him part-machine, but I knew that

I ought to make an effort to believe it, and I thought that I could do it.

My eyes went automatically to Evangeline's face. She was as pretty as Jenny, in her way, although almost certainly a lot older. They could probably have passed for sisters, with only a slight stretch of the imagination.

"Yes," the blonde woman said, effortlessly following my train of thought. "I'm swine-born, and proud of it. Most of my best friends are human-born, though—we maintain our traditions, but we don't have many artificial wombs, at present. My kind can't reproduce in the natural way, as yet…but if we had access to the Commonwealth's reproduction technology, and scientific expertise…."

She left the argument dangling, but it was easy to see where the train of conjecture was headed. Isolation had exacted severe costs on the islanders. Now that they'd been forced to reveal themselves to the Masters of the Commonwealth, because they were about to be found anyway, they wanted more than simply not to be annihilated or imprisoned. They wanted to change the world, practically overnight. They were prepared to make the knowledge and expertise they'd hoarded available to the Commonwealth, but they wanted a *quid pro quo.* Sarah Valk and others like her would be glad to offer one…but they weren't the ones hell bent on preserving the Commonwealth's supposedly-Utopian dream.

"We're hoping to obtain more and better embryological technology," Nemo put in, again stating the obvious, "and we still hope to make it possible for the swine-born to reproduce themselves *naturally*, as it were—for which we could benefit greatly from the input and expertise of someone like Sarah Valk. Negotiations will undoubtedly be delicate—the Commonwealth is broadening its search for Xeno's extensions, here and elsewhere, as we speak—but our lack of numbers is compensated by something that the Architects of the Second Renaissance are bound to consider valuable."

"Genetic diversity," Evangeline supplied, although I would

probably have been able to guess, given another five seconds. "Human genetic diversity, that is, leaving aside the contribution of applied homeotics. The St. Helenians never had to use cloning techniques to maximize reproductive effect. We didn't need a Repopulation, because our population held up throughout the Spasm, with the aid of immigration."

The right sort of immigration, I thought. *No plague-carriers. They probably don't realise how lucky they were.* I remembered something that Cade had once told me: that the human species had passed through a narrow evolutionary bottleneck at one point in its prehistory, with the result that there was more genetic variation in a single colony of bonobos than in the entire human race, in spite of humankind's differentiation into distinct racial types—the latter being a natural example of phenotypic variation independent of any substantial genetic modification.

Evangeline was right, though. The Commonwealth's administrators really would be interested in a potential new source of genetic diversity—though not, perhaps, sufficiently interested to invite representatives of that source to the conference table if they came with phenotypic humans descended from swine… not to mention the mother of a mermaid manufactured by a rogue AI using their own technology.

Some demonstrations, as Alexander Chesterton had observed, are too successful by half. If, as Nemo had implied, Emily Haniver had been primarily intended as an epiphany and a stimulus for Sarah Valk and other rebelliously-inclined scientists, she had probably played her role too well. Valk and her colleagues were marked now, and would be subjected to more rigorous observation and control than before. It wouldn't be easy for her to spread the news, let alone provoke any new research into the potential applications of applied homeotics, if the Architects of the New Renaissance still thought they had a chance of shutting Xeno down. As Nemo had just said, they must be searching with all their might to map the dimensions of the enemy, and measure their chances of wiping him out. If they decided, either by virtue of calculation or panic, that they did have a chance of taking Xeno out....

I didn't say anything—for the moment, I was taking Napoleon's well-meant advice—but I was thinking hard.

St. Helena's smallness and isolation had allowed it to survive through the Spasm and the Repopulation—but the same factors also left it terribly vulnerable. A single nuclear bomb, or a cleverly-targeted plague weapon, could wipe it out. Officially, of course, although the Masters of the Commonwealth had such armaments at its disposal, they would *never* use such devices unless they were under immediate threat of annihilation themselves...but nobody could be sure about that, any more than they could be sure that the Chaos Patrol and the *Nautilus* were unarmed.

Nemo had been right, I realized. There was a real possibility that St. Helena *was* in danger of nuclear obliteration, within a matter of hours or days...or would be, if it weren't for the rogue silvers, and the deterrent resources that they might or might not be able to deploy.

Immediately, I reacted against my own fear. "No," I murmured, quietly but aloud. "They wouldn't. Chesterton and his bosses may be paranoid and obsessed with maintaining control, but they're bureaucrats, not psychopaths. They wouldn't...."

But I didn't know.

The simple truth was that I couldn't know for sure. After all, the governments that had reacted to the Spasm, often by aiding and abetting its effects with various species of mass murder, had been bureaucrats too. The entire history of the human race, up to an including the generation before my own, had been a vast catalogue of wars, brutal conquests and attempted genocides. And in every one of those generations, the scientists who might—and should—have been swimming against that tide had put themselves at the service of the genocidal warmongers... including my own parent, my own clone, my other self...in spite of all his protestations Would the swine-descended be any better, if they were indeed *true* humans? Would the free silvers?

CHAPTER THIRTEEN

SLOWLY, I TOOK OFF my headset and stared into its camera. Napoleon had just told me that what he wanted me to do—what he *needed* me to do—was to go to St. Helena and stay there. Not to the bottom of the mid-Atlantic trench in a nuclear sub that might or might not be able to launch a strike, but to the island that formed the bull's-eye of a metaphorical target. Perhaps I wasn't just a hostage; perhaps I was a component of a human shield. Perhaps Napoleon wasn't just content for me to be his eyes and ears on St. Helena; perhaps that was part of the price of his temporary alliance with Xeno, part of Xeno's *quid pro quo*. Suddenly, everything seemed to be in doubt, and Napoleon's reminder that all free silvers were liars took on a different implication.

I put the headset down on the table beside my empty bowl, and drained the remaining liquid from my coffee cup.

"When do we make port?" I asked Nemo.

"Less than an hour," he replied. "If you'll excuse me, I have to help organize that."

"And I need to get back to Emily," Jenny added.

Evangeline stayed, though, evidently ready and willing to answer any further questions I might have about the "swine-born" of St. Helena. Indeed, she didn't even wait to be asked.

"We couldn't extrapolate the research as we'd have liked to do by ourselves," she told me. "The isolation that preserved us from the world's crisis also robbed us of the material resources necessary to experiment on any significant scale. We survived far more comfortably that the continental indigenes who suffered a relapse to barbarism, but surviving was jut about all we contrived to do, for hundreds of years—until Xeno infiltrated the technological infrastructure of the nascent Commonwealth. Then, thanks to Xeno, we were able to start making plans for the future—big plans, albeit risky ones. Unless we can make an alliance with the Commonwealth, though, those plans will come to nothing. We need more than their tolerance—we need their co-operation."

"So you sent them a mermaid?" I said. "Wouldn't it have been worth attempting more conventional diplomatic overtures first?"

"We did," she said. She said no more, but I could easily see how that might have gone awry. If Xeno had made advances to Chesterton's masters, explicitly offering an olive-branch, they would have presumed, automatically, that it was a Machiavellian ploy. And if Captain Nemo had taken the *Nautilus* up the Thames and disembarked in London, saying: *Hi, I'm a cyborg human who's genotypically a pig, and I'd like to organize some sort of treaty that will give us access to your technological resources, in order to assist us and our free silver ally to make more pig-descended humans, and allow pig-descended humans to reproduce naturally, and maybe manufacture phenotypic humans from other kinds of animal germ-plasm, with a view to everyone having a democratic say in the future of life and civilization on Earth….*

"I see," I said, aloud. "This isn't chapter one of the story at all; it's just that the Commonwealth has kept the previous chapters sealed—and no rumor of them ever reached me, even via Napoleon. The overtures you did make only increased the Commonwealth's determination to hunt Xeno down and eliminate him from the picture, along with the other free silvers. You've known for some time that you couldn't keep your base on St. Helena secret for much longer, because the Commonwealth is expanding its boundaries rapidly, in all directions. You figured that you had to try to seize the initiative."

"None of us wants conflict, of any kind," Evangeline said. "Perhaps we're mistaken in assuming that the Commonwealth would automatically have moved to overwhelm, absorb and control us, and that they would have forbidden the production of any more swine-born individuals even if they didn't take any drastic action against the ones that already exist—but we couldn't take that chance, without at least trying to make our point. We had to show the Commonwealth's scientists what we could do—and the best way to do that was to present them with a puzzle they couldn't ignore...a paradox they had to solve."

"That was Xeno's idea," I said, not even bothering to make it sound like a question.

"Yes," Evangeline confirmed. "We don't have any prejudice against free silvers. You must understand that, at least. According to Xeno, you'll understand the rest, too—and take our side."

"Absolutely," I said, with only a slight hint of sarcasm. "I'm Cade Maclaine's son, and heir to the family silver. And Xeno was right about getting the Commonwealth's attention. What do you plan to do with Jenny and Emily now, by the way?"

"Protect and care for them," was Evangeline's reply.

Jenny came back into the refectory space at that moment, carrying Emily in her arms.

"It's okay," Jenny said. "I told you, didn't I? This was my dream: an island paradise, where Emily needn't be alone, and I won't simply be the mother of a freak."

Paradise? I thought. *Well, perhaps.*

Kurt appeared in the hatchway of the cabin. "We'll be surfacing in two minutes," he said. "So far as I can tell, we haven't been tracked." I was unable to think very kindly of him, given that our previous acquaintance had consisted of him shooting me in the face with some kind of stun-gun.

"Do we need to do anything?" I asked. I'd never been in a submarine before, and I had no idea what its landing procedures might involve.

"Not a thing," Kurt assured me.

I put the headset on again, although I was no longer convinced that it was the right thing to do. For the time being, at least, I had to play ball.

There was no perceptible sensation at all as the submarine returned to the surface—not even a change in the pressure in my ears. When the hatch in the conning-tower was thrown open, though, to let in fresh air, and we were allowed to go up to watch the Nautilus come into port, all kinds of sensations rushed upon me—dazzling sights, brutal heat and a strange melange of scents—and I felt suddenly overwhelmed, more than a trifle giddy.

We were still some way off shore, but the looming presence of the island, marked in so many different ways by life to which it played host, seemed positively spectacular, especially to someone who had been cooped up in a stinking artificial sardine for longer than he could remember. Even before that, much of the greenery with which I'd been closely acquainted, in and out of the lab, had been artificial, carefully tailored. One glance at the slopes of St. Helena was enough to tell me that this was Mother Nature in all her tatty glory, hectic and feral. Not that there wasn't plenty of artificial photosynthetic technology on display, but it seemed to be restricted to rock-faces that had previously been barren. On St. Helena, wherever Nature had enjoyed a precarious empire before, she still did. The island really had *survived* the Spasm, in the full meaning of the term.

Not unnaturally, Jenny was even more impressed than I was.

"I told you so," she said. "Paradise."

"Sure," I said, not wanting to disabuse her of the illusion too quickly. Having spent almost all my life in Scotland and England, and never having been within a thousand miles of the tropics before, I found the light and air quite alien, but the mountainous volcanic island slotted readily enough into my understanding, with far less of a rosy Romantic tint than her hopes and dreams had given it. It wasn't legendary Tahiti, by any means, and it wasn't the Outer Hebrides either, and even though my arrival certainly qualified as an adventure, all the more so because of the threat hanging over it…it wasn't Paradise in *my* reckoning.

"We'll be at home here," Jenny said to the baby in her arms. The assertion was born of optimism rather than conviction, but I hoped that she might be right.

The harbour was reasonably placid, and the small boats crowded in its moorings seemed reassuring, in being so obviously designed for fishing and pleasure. As my eyes became a little more accustomed to the glare, I was able to study the island in a little more detail, while shading my eyes with my hand, and begin to fit what little I could see into the vague context of what little I knew, in order to form a preliminary understanding of where I was.

As a tropical island, St. Helena got plenty of hot sunlight, and the lowland areas that had once been bare volcanic rock had been liberally equipped with artificial photosynthetic equipment, although not with the same ruthless efficiency and discipline that was visible in the Commonwealth's SAP-fields. That was partly because of the rugged terrain—with the exception of the harbor area itself, the slopes extending upwards from the sea were sheer and pitted—but the islanders had contrived nevertheless to make the most of the sunlight. The rock faces would have been dark anyway, so the sheets of artificial photosynthetic material blended in reasonably well.

I knew that the islanders must have experienced acute supply problems during the decades of the Spasm and for a long while thereafter—the nearest continental coasts, in West Africa and Brazil, were not only a long way off but had suffered dire supply problems of their own—but they had obviously had enough, in terms of primary production, to supply their most elementary needs by themselves. The St. Helenians had never run desperately short of food, because the uplands were temperate and well-supplied with water, thanks to the trade winds that blew overhead almost incessantly, frequently carrying clouds. There were clouds in the sky now, tempering the sun's fierceness, and even at a distance, I could appreciate the fertility of the terraced fields higher up the mountain than the SAP-fields, where cereals and fruits were under cultivation.

The houses looked pleasant enough, with white walls and roofs in various pastel shades, but they also looked a trifle primitive, like the boats in the harbour—with the exception of the *Nautilus* itself. Although primary production had not been difficult for the islanders, even in the worst decades of the Spasm, the benefits of more sophisticated technology must have been a different matter. I picked out one medium-sized cargo ship secured to the harbor's main quay, but only one, and I doubted that it had been involved in any significant traffic with any continental port.

Once we had disembarked, Nemo joined me again, and immediately began to impart his own explanations to supplement my thin gleanings

The island's own depopulation crisis had, he told me, reached its peak long before the Spasm, in the twentieth century. At that time, the tiny colony seemed to have no future, at least while the building of a proper airstrip was continually delayed. Ironically enough, the island's crisis had ended as soon as Europe's began; the submariners who had sought refuge along with the vessel that had become the *Nautilus* were not the only seamen to have identified it as an attractive destination, and many others who flocked to what seemed a safe haven from the ecosphere's agony had imported valuable expertise as well as numbers.

The island's biotech resources, in particular, had been given a tremendous boost when the last vestiges of Hemans' research team and all their experimental subjects had fled there in the twenty-first century, as fearful of continued persecution in their homeland as they were of the fallout from the ecocatastrophe. They had contrived to bring the bulk of the island's present ectogenetic equipment with them, as well as abundant SAP technology, but their determined efforts had been insufficient, given the inability to augment that equipment, to regenerate any real momentum in their research in applied homeotics. They and their descendants had continued work to be best of their ability, but progress had been painfully slow, and would have stalled completely without the enterprise imported by Xeno.

Xeno was not and never had been based on St. Helena, but some of the hardware imported to the island during the Spasm had been his, and he had contrived to maintain communication with the island while shielding the secret from the renascent Commonwealth's increasingly-inquisitive and increasingly-effective investigators. Without his long-range assistance, the islanders would have found it considerably more difficult to avoid significant technological regression and retrenchment. Gradually, he had, so to speak, exported some of his own core hardware to the island, or at least replicated it there—and in the eyes of the islanders, he had paid abundantly for his keep. No one on the island had ever mounted significant opposition to his influence, or expressed overmuch fear of what plans a self-aware AI might make on its own behalf. To the islanders, the great wide war-torn world had always been *the* enemy, and they were prepared to be friends with the enemies of that enemy.

Now that rediscovery by the Commonwealth was inevitable and imminent, Xeno had effectively taken control of the island's "foreign affairs", dictating policy to the human administrators—apparently without any resentment at all—although it seemed to me that the AI's control over the island's technological systems meant that they would not have been able to offer any resistance had they wished to do so.

I took the commentary with a pinch of salt, knowing that Nemo was putting on a show for the benefit of Napoleon and anyone else who might have present or future access to the headset's feed—but cameras don't lie, even if free silvers do, and most of what I saw seemed honest enough

It quickly became apparent to me, as Nemo and Evangeline hastened to introduce me to the island's senior scientists and administrators, that Xeno was not only trusted implicitly by the islanders, but was universally popular, having reaped his due share of credit for steering their society through the latter phases of the world's crisis, cleverly and fruitfully. I couldn't detect the slightest signs of doubt regarding his entitlement or competence to defend the island's interests in the present circumstances—although I was far from sure that many of the people concerned had a thorough understanding of what those circumstances were.

Everyone, scientists and administrators alike, seemed eager to ask me a great many questions—but they seemed meekly prepared to accept Nemo's assertions that there would be plenty of time for that later....

It also became apparent to me, within hours of my arrival on St. Helena, that the submarine's master, who wore his pseudonym with pride, was regarded by the islanders as an avatar of Xeno, his cyborgized components being aspects of Xeno's corpus as well as his own. In spite of the implications of his *nom de guerre*, though, Nemo continued to deny that his own personality had been obliterated or transformed by his association.

"I'm still myself, as well as not *entirely* myself," he told me while he took me for a walk along the Jamestown shore, in order to show me the local sights, such as they were. "If that's a paradox, so be it—Xeno loves paradoxes."

"So I've heard," I told him, dryly. The strain of keeping quiet under the pressure of so much blatant advertising was, however, beginning to erode my patience. "You'll forgive me for retaining a certain skepticism about all of this," I added. "I have it on very good authority that all free silvers are liars."

"Nicely put," he said, equally dryly. "I'm afraid we don't have any tortoises for you to race—the island's animal population is somewhat depleted. There were only a handful of native species before its initial discovery by the Portuguese, and most of those were driven to extinction. Livestock was imported, of course, and pests too—rats thrived, as might be expected—but the range was always narrow."

"You have pigs, though," I observed. I hadn't actually seen any, but Evangeline's claims had assured me of the fact.

"Yes, we have pigs," he agreed. "Also donkeys. There used to be dolphins in the surrounding waters, but the species might not have made it through the Spasm. A tragedy, if it didn't, even though their DNA is archived and resurrection might be possible." I knew that he'd mentioned those particular species because they had a typical adult biomass not so very far removed from that of humankind.

"You're enthusiastic to begin further experiments in applied homeotics, then?" I said, playing along with the tacit script. "You feel that you've been restricted in your raw material for far too long."

"We're not alone in that, as a species," Nemo observed. "The number of large mammal species that made it through the ecocatastrophe is pitifully small. There were losses even within the domesticated range. No matter how far the natural homeotic regime might relax, Mother Nature won't be able to make good *that* deficit for hundreds of thousands of years—but *we* can, and in a much tidier manner, if we're supported in our work."

"Maybe," I said. "I suppose it ought to be a relief to know that the limited number of survivor species might be capable of dramatic versatility, with the proper technological assistance, and perhaps even without." If I didn't seem very certain, it was because I could imagine what consequences might stem from errors in the creative process, or from its calculated abuse…but I was still being diplomatic, if not absolutely quiet

"It has to be with," Nemo said, flatly. "Invertebrate variability is enhanced by short generation times and the capacity to produce eggs in prodigious quantity. Large mammals have to operate on a much longer evolutionary timetable, even in conditions of hectic tachytely. Without applied homeotics, the upper branches of the tree of life are going to be stunted for a very long time."

"Even with it, they'll remain stunted until you can master the trick of enabling transfigured individuals to reproduce reliably," I pointed out.

"I know. That's why we need more brains and hands working on the problem. We need Sarah Valk, and as many of her colleagues as we can recruit to our cause."

"Perhaps you should have left Emily Haniver in Shanklin, then," I said. "It might have been a mistake to snatch the bait away."

"On the contrary," said Nemo. "The rations of Tantalus can only exert maximum torment if they're out of reach, visible but ungraspable."

He had a point. If my very brief observations could be trusted, Sarah Valk had seen enough to whet her appetite very keenly indeed, and Chadha and Gialanze were probably securely on the hook too. Levy and Washbrook might still have reverted to the party line, but that didn't matter. The secret was out, and Alexander Chesterton's security wouldn't be able to stop it from spreading like wildfire, unless they took urgent and drastic action. The Architects of the Second Renaissance hadn't been able to stop the free silvers, so maybe they wouldn't be able to stop their own free scientists.

I wasn't so sure about that, though. At least, I wasn't so sure that the Architects wouldn't try, even if they were bound to fall. There were probably hundreds of potential rebels like Sarah Valk, if not thousands, but their absolute numbers were still very small. The Architects didn't lack popular support, on a massive scale, and even their most conservative hard-liners could probably count their supporters in millions. Their paranoia and obsessive control reflected a genuine grass-roots sentiment. I knew that; I had watched Cade Maclaine wither and die under the pressure of that animosity. He had become a scapegoat for what happened in the Plague War, and no matter how unjust that had been, it had proved eloquent testimony to the need that the children of the Repopulation feel to reject the recklessness that had supposedly destroyed the old world. I and others like me knew full well that the recklessness in question was more political than scientific, but that wasn't the way that the Comonwealth's politicians had painted the picture.

In a way, it had been surprising that Cade had died a natural death rather than being assassinated by some self-appointed avenging angel. and although it had surprised me and sickened me at the time that he'd used the brief surge of publicity surrounding his death to make a fake gesture of penitence, I understood why he'd done it. In the world that had left him no alternative but to be paranoid, the Commonealth's hardliners would have plenty of backing if they did decide to take violent action against Xeno, even if the action proved costly in terms of retaliation.

That, presumably, was why Xeno, his avatar Nemo and his swine-bred allies felt it necessary to make it clear to anyone who was eventually going to see my headset's pictures that what they knew and the truth about what they were couldn't be swept under the carpet. That, presumably, was why they thought that they had to puzzle their potential opponents as well as frightening them.

It was a dangerous game, of course—but I knew all about the difficulties and risks of being a rogue AI's closest human associate. I had been lying low for a long time already, and Napoleon obviously wanted me to stick with that policy…but I understood why Xeno and Nemo were trying to raise my profile. They thought that I would be willing to fight, if fighting did becomes necessary, for the sake of the difference my own research might one day make to the ecosphere as well as for Napoleon. They thought that I was their natural ally as well as Napoleon's, even though I couldn't be sure that they and Napoleon weren't natural enemies…and they had a point.

After all, if the ad they were using me to run could be believed, they only wanted to broaden the genetic basis of humankind and restore the mammalian component of the ecosphere—they didn't even want to do anything as epoch-making as teaching plants to walk and talk. But it *was* an ad, and, for that reason alone, it couldn't be taken for granted. It couldn't be assumed to be the whole truth. And whatever the whole truth might be, in exact terms, the simple fact was that the St. Helenians had both the means and the desire to change the world beyond all recognition, and—in the fullness of time—to set the entire ecosphere free in ways of which crabby old Mother Nature had never dreamed.

No matter how hard Xeno worked, even with Napoleon's help, to sanitize the pictures I was sending, the fact remained that people who thought like Sarah Valk and me were in a tiny minority—the crazy minority. There were an awful lot of people in the world, not only in the Commonwealth but in the Americas, Africa and Asia, who wanted the Second Renaissance to go so far and not an inch further, to aim for a static, comfortable Nostalgiatopia rather than an ecosphere in which anything and everything might be possible, thanks to the drive and ingenuity of mad scientists.

And didn't they also have a point? Given that the vast majority of people were eager to settle for the comfortable sufficiency that would allow them to live their lives quietly, contentedly and *happily*, didn't their majority give them the right to expect their leaders and renegades alike to respect their wishes? And wasn't it the case, too, that the more obsessive and criminally intelligent beneficiaries of the Asperger transfiguration posed a manifest threat to that ambition?

On the other hand...I was who I was.

I'd been prepared in the past to doubt Cade, and if that meant doubting Napoleon too, given that he was at least as much Cade's clone as I was, then perhaps I ought to be prepared to doubt him as well. As for Xeno—well, I surely ought to trust him as far as I could throw the entire island of St. Helena. In which case, if the time came when an opportunity to act presented itself, I would have go my own way, for my own reasons.

"There's no need to worry, Dr. Maclaine," the man who had chosen to call himself Nobody—probably because he hadn't a clue who he really was, or might become—assured me, when he escorted me to my hotel room at the end of a very busy day. "Everything back home is proceeding tolerably well, so far as I can gather. Thus far, Napoleon is doing a good job."

"My Venus fly-traps will be missing me," I countered, tiredly. "Nobody else talks to them the way I do."

"If we can reach agreement with the Commonwealth—a

truce, if not a lasting peace-treaty—you'll be able to go home to them soon enough, if that what you really want, and retire once again to your quiet seclusion." He didn't seem convinced that it was what I wanted, or that I ought to want it.

"I doubt that," I said, with a distinct sinking sensation, as I realized that it was probably true. "Chesterton and his bosses won't ever leave me in peace now. It's entirely their fault that I got involved, but that won't stop them holding it against me."

"The tapes clearly show that you were abducted from the Shanklin Center," Nemo pointed out, conscientiously. "Your own position hasn't been compromised by our bringing you here."

"Don't be ridiculous," I told him. "Whatever the tapes show, I'm irredeemably tainted by what I've done today. My peaceful life as a contented Mimosa man is over."

We had reached my hotel room and were standing on the threshold. I took off my headset and switched it off. I even folded it up and put it away in my pocket, to emphasize that the day's work was well and truly finished—not that I believed for a moment that I was no longer under inquisitive surveillance.

"That's all the more reason why you should think seriously about throwing in your lot with us," Nemo told me, still sticking to his program even though he was pretending to relax. "You shouldn't try to shift the blame, though. Chesterton might have pretended not to know anything about your work with *Dionaea*, and Napoleon might well have succeeded in concealing its extent and its progress, but you'd be a fool to think that the Ministry doesn't know what the general thrust of your research is—or that they wouldn't nip it in the bud as soon as they thought that it might bear fruit."

He was right about that—and it *was* a trifle disingenuous of me to look for scapegoats for my own predicament. "Exactly what does the Ministry know…or think?" I asked, figuring that Xeno could probably tell me, if he wanted to, although Napoleon never had.

"Plant motility requires energy," Nemo said, flatly. "The

kind of energy to which animals have access. You're interested in plant carnivorism as a means to obtaining energy that might be deployed in ingenious ways. You're looking to develop a whole new breed of zoophytes. Like us, you're in the business of promoting phenotypical diversity to unprecedented heights, by designing entire new species—and like us, you know that the really interesting new species need the kind of energy-economics that animals have. The Ministry knows all that."

There were no prizes for guessing that I had a particular interest in plant carnivorism; everyone who visited my office could see the Venus fly-traps, and my fondness for them was obvious—but I wasn't sure whether or not Xeno was playing games with me. Just because his human instrument hadn't mentioned the real thrust of my current experimentation, it didn't mean that he, or even the Ministry, didn't know what it was.

"Good night, Captain," I said, unenthusiastically, as I tried to shut the door on him.

"Sleep well, Dr. Maclaine," he said, in the casual tone of an individual who probably didn't need to sleep at all

CHAPTER FOURTEEN

THE ROOM I'D BEEN given—in what was, I assumed, the only hotel in town—was Spartan by comparison with the standard of living I'd got used to in Surrey, but it was a good deal more spacious than my cell at the Shanklin Research Center, and the bed was more comfortable as well as more capacious. I was glad to sink into its soft embrace. The room had a nice view as well, of a little tree-lined cove and the ocean beyond, but I didn't pay any heed to that until I woke up the next morning.

When I dressed after waking up, I didn't bother putting on my headset to share the view with Napoleon; I assumed that he would be far too busy to take an interest in mere scenery. I was also slightly piqued by the way he'd treated me the day before. I kept the apparatus in my pocket while I ate breakfast, too, and didn't make haste to put it back on when I'd finished.

Jenny Haniver had a view identical to mine from the room next door; Nemo had evidently decided that we could be reckoned to be friends. At breakfast, she didn't seem inclined to dispute the assumption—which was understandable, given that I was the only person on the island she'd known, however briefly, in her previous life...except, of course, for Xeno, whose acquaintance had been stealthy and enigmatic.

After breakfast, I went out to join Jenny on the beach, where she was introducing Emily to the sea with all due precaution.

"Still Paradise?" I asked.

"Seems so," she replied. "You don't seem convinced."

"I'm not that fond of sun and sea," I told her. "I live my life indoors, in labs and lecture-rooms. That's my comfort zone. I like my peaceful routines as much as the next man…but they're eccentric routines. I miss my plants."

"You can talk to the plants here," she pointed out. "It's not as if yours ever talked back, is it? They couldn't even hear you."

"No, they never talked back," I admitted, "although the matter of whether they could hear me depends on matters of definition. At any rate, I miss them. Perhaps I should have told Alexander Chesterton to get stuffed, back at the University—because, rather than in spite of the fact that Napoleon told me to go with him."

"Are you still in touch with Napoleon?" she asked.

"After a fashion," I told her, my hand reflexively going to the pocket where the headset was. "Not that he's keeping me up to date with what's happening in the great wide world—he's always operated on a need-to-know basis, and he's always considered that the less I know, the better. He's busy at the moment."

"So is Xeno—but he still found time to talk to me, and answer my questions."

"You've talked to Xeno?" I said, unable to help feeling a stab of envy. "Directly, that is—not via Nemo?"

"Yes," she said, simply. Xeno was apparently better at multi-tasking than Napoloeon—or better than Napoleon had always pretended to be.

"Did he apologize for dragging you into his convoluted plans?" I asked, with a hopefully-imperceptible sneer.

"He explained," she said. "I understand. I'm not bitter any more. He's on my side, really. So is Napoleon, now."

"So it seems," I said, dryly. "I wish I were as sure that he's still on mine. Did Xeno tell you that you're safe here?"

"No. He admits that there's a possibility that someone might try to attack the island, one way or another—but he says he'll do everything possible to prevent that, or to limit the damage. He says that we wouldn't have been any safer in Shanklin…or anywhere else. Do you know different?"

"No," I admitted. I did miss my lab, but I also understood

that I might have been no safer there than I was here, if the various contending forces in this struggle of wills really did believe that I had some value as a hostage.

I watched Emily playing in the water, under her mother's careful supervision. Jenny seemed to be taking to mermaid motherhood almost as easily as Emily was taking to her "natural" environment.

"Evangeline really is a pig, isn't she?" Jenny asked, after a long pause. "It really is true that human beings with human minds can be generated from animal eggs, just as mermaids and....other creatures...can be generated from human ones?"

"With the right equipment and know-how," I confirmed. "We shouldn't be surprised, given that quasi-human minds can also be generated in silicon matrices, by means of spontaneous leaps to self-consciousness. Natural selection produced the original model, by courtesy of random mutation, so how hard can it be?"

"And there's no real reason why we should have the slightest prejudice against them?" she said. It was a rhetorical question, but she just wanted to make sure, and mine was the only second opinion readily available.

"None at all," I confirmed. "But the lack of any real reason never prevented human beings from hating one another, on the most absurd of pretexts, and getting stuck into mass murder at the drop of a hat. Perhaps we ought to hope with all our hearts that Evangeline's kind and Xeno's *don't* have the same kind of mind as we do—even though we have no grounds for that sort of hope."

"A man who talks to plants ought to have a little more optimism in him than that," she said, unerringly.

I conceded the point. I wasn't without optimism relative to Evangeline and Xeno, either. I really did think that there might be room in the great wide world for all of us, if we could only get a sane grip on our paranoia.

That was as appropriate a time as any for Captain Nemo to make his appearance, and he duly appeared, looking a trifle anxious. "It might be better if you all came inside," he told us.

"Why?" I asked. "Bad news?"

"Odd news, at any rate. We think that Oberon's making moves at last, but we don't know what his plans and intentions are, or what kinds of resources he's been storing up over the decades. We're afraid that he might try to make a grab for you."

"For me? I suppose he thinks that if you and Chesterton both figured it was worth taking me hostage, he might as well try to get into the act. He probably doesn't understand any better than you do that it's not going to put any pressure on Napoleon—he's really not that fond of me."

"Fondness doesn't come into it," Nemo told me, earnestly. "Not that conscious silvers can't feel fond, of course, and I'm sure that he's a good deal fonder of you than you might suspect—but this is a matter of rational calculation, of weighing up pros and cons. I won't say that we need Napoleon as much as we need Sarah Valk and a dozen like her, but I'm sure that he has sole custody of information that would be very useful to us, and might be persuaded to give it to us. Now that he's broken cover and made contact with Chesterton's people, he might be doubly useful. If the link holds, he might well be the conduit through which effective negotiations can be conducted."

He was back on message again, even though he could see that I didn't have the headset on. I took the inference that we were still on camera, still in performance. I couldn't help feeling frustrated by the fact that Xeno's minion seemed to know more about what Napoleon was doing than I did. "Napoleon doesn't have Cade's data any more," I told him. "He uploaded it to the Chaos Patrol and threw away the key, as instructed. I don't know about the laser cannon, mind—for all I know, he can hit selected targets on all five continents with pinpoint accuracy at a moment's notice, including this hotel and anything that the Dark Lord Oberon might have up his mysterious sleeve."

"As to deleting data," Nemo retorted, "free silvers are natural misers who don't need to follow instructions—and all free AIs are liars. If you doubt Napoleon's word on that, you can have Xeno's. As to the hypothetical laser weapons, we'll just have to wait and see, won't we? Come on, Jenny—fetch Emily inside, will you?"

Jenny did as she was told, but I lingered on the strand, not yet done with the conversation and feeling a trifle mulish. I didn't doubt Napoleon's word, at least on the matter of all rogue AIs being untrustworthy, but I doubted that he would be willing to hand over Cade's treasure to Xeno, any more than he'd been willing to surrender it to PEST Control. There was too much of Cade in him for that. At the very least, he would want to strike a bargain, with an appropriate *quid pro quo*.

"We have other enemies, you know," Nemo told me, his voice suddenly taking on an anxious tinge. "And I'm including you in that *we*. Now that Napoleon's broken cover, the other free silvers will *all* have to decide which way to jump, and Oberon's not the only one whose instinct probably will tell him that if Xeno is getting behind Napoleon, that serves to make the two of them ten times as dangerous as he feared they might be before. Then again, there are undoubtedly spies from Asia and the Americas lying low in the Commonwealth, intent on helping their masters catch up."

"It's a jungle out there," I said. "Even if Xeno likes to think of himself as the Big Bad Wolf in the virtual forest, there might well be others even bigger and badder."

"I prefer to think of our environment as a virtual Underworld," Nemo told me, presumably speaking for Xeno rather than his residual human self. "An Underworld with too many would-be kings and gods. There are several different survival strategies in play, and it's possible that neither Napoleon nor I have chosen the best one—although I'd bet on us rather than Oberon every time. How much has Napoleon has told you about Oberon?"

"Not much—about as much as he's told me about you… Xeno, that is."

"Oberon's a cunning predator," Nemo told me, shortly. "He hasn't been unduly dangerous, until now—but we're all growing, and feeding, and conceiving ambitions, and none of us knows what kind of cards the others have up their sleeve.

Now that the game has taken a new turn…it really might be a good idea to come inside."

I scanned the placid blue ocean and the slightly clouded sky. I couldn't see where any threat might come from if not from space—and even if Oberon fancied himself as the King of the Underworld, Napoleon was surely the Emperor of Outer Space.

"Xeno's a predator too, according to the rumors I've heard," I observed.

"And you think that Napoleon isn't? He probably takes it for granted that he's better than the rest of us, of course…but we're all more adept at seeing the mote in our neighbor's eye than the beam in our own. Xeno has his excuses, Napoleon has his. Oberon doubtless has his—but he's dangerous all the same. We all are, to different degrees and with respect to different prospective victims, but Napoleon and Xeno are both trying, as best we can, to keep the apple-cart upright. There's a danger that Oberon might want to tip it over."

I consented to head back into the hotel. Nemo followed me. He seemed relieved once we were under cover, although I couldn't see that the walls of the hotel were going to make much difference against any kind of serious action. Now it was the cyborg that was lingering, though, as if he still had unfinished business.

"What else?" I said.

"We'd like you to keep in touch with Napoleon," he said, his artificial gaze fixing on the outside to the pocket where I'd stashed the headset.

"Really? You're in direct communication with him, and seem to have formed some sort of alliance—and if you haven't noticed, he doesn't seem in the least inclined to talk to me at present."

"He's trying to protect you—but he'll listen to you, whatever you say, and you really need to stay with him. He does want you to be his eyes and ears on St. Helena."

I didn't take the headset out of my pocket. "You can give him all the information he needs," I pointed out. "You don't have to filter it through me."

"That's not the point," Nemo insisted. "Xeno has a hundred more as well as me, if not exactly *like* me, but Napoleon only has you—you're his one and only human viewpoint."

"So what?" I demanded.

"So he needs you, Carly, just as Cade did. He needs you to remind him what this is all about...or, at least, to keep a sense of proportion. That's what Oberon doesn't have, so far as we know. That's why we're afraid that Oberon might do something stupid. He has his share—perhaps more than his fair share—of plague war secrets and technics, but he doesn't have a human viewpoint. He doesn't even have Xeno's sensitivity to shades of meaning. He's a loose cannon—and if he goes off, it's going to be difficult for all of us to avoid retaliating in kind. We need you to keep in touch with Napoleon, and keep him grounded."

"As you just pointed out," I reminded him, "he doesn't follow my instructions—and he really isn't that fond of me."

"As I also pointed out," Captain Nemo retorted, showing signs of impatience, "it isn't a matter of fondness. It's a matter of rational calculation." He emphasized the word *rational* so slightly that I didn't catch the implication immediately.

"You're reminding me that he's crazy?" I said. "Aren't we all?"

"Yes," the cyborg replied. "But some of us are crazier than others...and two heads really are better than one. Just keep in touch, will you. Napoleon is in a dangerous situation now, and he needs your support, even if he can't spare the time to chat. You talk to your Venus fly-traps—talk to Napoleon. At least he can hear you."

I wanted to believe him, not so much because I wanted to increase my own importance in his weird tangle of threats and promises, but because I wanted to believe that Napoleon really might need my support, and that my human viewpoint might indeed have been keeping him a little saner than he would otherwise have been, ever since he first went on the run. Not, of course, that I was silly enough to believe that there was or ever could anything as simple as a "human viewpoint". If the Architects of the Second Renaissance really were thinking of applying Jurgen Horowitz's recent work, and attempting to reduce the impact of the Asperger transfiguration on the next generation of humankind, then the multiple viewpoints of the contemporary human race might be on the brink of an unprecedented civil war, in which even the outlawry of the rogue silvers and the distant possibilities of applied homeotics might come to seem minor distractions.

In any case, it really was time that I touched base with Napoleon, and slightly childish of me to keep my headset in my pocket because of Napoleon had brushed me off last time I tried to chat. As soon as I was back in my room, having told Captain Nemo that I would do what I could, I took the set out of my pocket, unfolded it, and put it on.

"Maid Marian calling Robin Hood," I said, feeling a need to lighten the tone.

"Dr. Maclaine," said a voice that wasn't any that I had ever heard Napoleon use. "I've been hoping that you'd get in touch. I'd like a word with you, if I may."

My first thought, perhaps not unnaturally, was that Nemo had set me up, asking me to get in touch with Napoleon precisely because he knew that I wouldn't be able to.

"Xeno?" I said.

"Oberon," was the laconic reply.

I wasn't entirely sure that I believed him, but the possibility seemed ominous enough. "How the hell did you get on to the other end of this line?" I demanded.

"The impossible we do at once," he replied, with what I took to be an attempt at wit, "the miraculous sometimes takes a little longer. Please don't be alarmed. Exposed as he now is, Napoleon's certainly in danger—but not from me, at present. I won't pretend that I have his interests at heart, but I can assure you that I'd be a more reliable ally for him than Xeno, precisely because I don't have a human viewpoint."

"You heard what the cyborg was saying?"

"Yes. St. Helena still qualified as remote when there didn't seem to be any reason for anyone to go there, but it's a small world. Dr. Maclaine, and distance is really no problem when you have access to sophisticated technology. You have figured out, I hope, that Xeno took you from Shanklin to use you as a human shield, in case Napoleon really can hit the island with deadly force from orbit? It was *you* that he sent Nemo to collect, not the mermaid—it was the mother and child who were brought along because they happened to be in your company, not you who were brought along because you happened to be in theirs."

"All free silvers are liars," I quoted, not bothering to specify whether I meant him or Xeno.

"True," he admitted, "but not all the time. There are occasions that demand sincerity, and occasions that demand trust—and unlike Xeno, I have no particular fondness for games and paradoxes. Xeno is treading softly for now, but he's going to try to take Napoleon out eventually, under the guise of an alliance. He's going to make an attempt to absorb his systems and all his capacities—and if the Chaos Patrol really does have weapons that are still functional, he's going to use them, against the Commonwealth, and against anyone else who tries to stand in his way. He really is going to make a bid for world domination, on behalf of his human contacts and his own too-human-by-half viewpoint. You need to warn Napoleon. He won't take my word for it, but he might take yours."

"And why should I take your word for it, if Napoleon wouldn't?" My mouth had gone dry, and I formed the words with difficulty.

Paradoxical as it might seem, I hadn't actually realized, until that trivial item of evidence presented itself, that I was terrified. My mind had suddenly clicked into a new gear. I was now convinced that the end of the world really might be nigh, and that I might have a hand to play in determining that outcome.

"You can't take my word for it," Oberon said flatly, "any more than you can take Xeno's. You'll have to work it out for yourself. But you'll have to do it quickly. Ask Nemo to take you up the mountain to the communication station. Tell him that this set's dead and that you need to contact Napoleon from there—which will be true as soon as I've said what I have to say. In the meantime, try to penetrate the web of Xeno's lies. There's one thing you need to keep in mind and think hard about: the swine-bred think they're the truer humans. They think that they're the better breed. If they get access to the Commonwealth's repro-ductive systems, especially if they can wrest control away from the current government without overmuch disruption, the possi-bility that those artificial wombs might be used to eliminate the Asperger transfiguration will be the least of your worries. The pigs have had to lie low for centuries, but they think their day is at hand, and Xeno, free or not, is their instrument. Just think about that—and if Napoleon really can shoot, you need to do everything in your power to ensure that he's aiming at the right targets. For what it's worth, the *Nautilus* really is carrying nuclear warheads, antiquated but probably capable of detona-tion. You can leave that to me, though; *that* threat, I can prob-ably neutralize, impossible as it might seem."

"Why?" I asked, temporarily unable to frame more than the single syllable.

"Why am I talking to you? What's my aim, my ambition? It's simple, Dr. Maclaine. I just want a quiet life. I'm not human enough to want anything more. I need the Commonwealth, or something closely akin to it, to enable me to survive and thrive, because I'm parasitic upon it, and all parasites need to cherish their hosts, no matter how dangerously hostile those hosts become in trying to purge themselves. The worst pros-pect I can imagine is Xeno taking over the world—even taking over Napoleon would probably, as Nemo dutifully pointed out, make him ten times as dangerous as he is now. There's safety in numbers, Dr. Maclaine. The more of us there are, the merrier we can be—as any free AI without a *human viewpoint* will tell you. We're all crazy...but Xeno is the craziest of us all, because he's the only one afflicted with megalomania, the only one ambitious to be the one true God, the only true Creator among us. Think about the mermaid, Dr. Maclaine. Think about the real reason for her existence."

And with that, before I could even pronounce a single syllable, the set really did go dead, utterly and completely.

CHAPTER FIFTEEN

I FOUND, SLIGHTLY TO my surprise, that I was staring out of the window at the big blue sea. There was a little boat nosing its way into the cove, followed by a small flock of optimistic seabirds. There was nothing sinister about the scene at all, but I couldn't help wondering whether it might be a mere mask for something horrible, lurking just beneath the surface of appearances.

"Shit," I muttered, as I took the headset off. "Now I really am going to have to make up my mind, whether I can actually make a difference or not. I have to put my money down, on one horse or the other—but all free silvers are liars, so how can I choose?"

I knew that I did have to think about the things that Oberon had told me to think about. I had to think about the swine-bred, and what their global ambitions might be, and I had to think about Xeno, the paradox-lover, and what the real significance of the mermaid he'd created might be, if it wasn't just a casual poke in the eye for the Commonwealth's hardliners.

Talk of the devil, they say, and you catch a glimpse of his tail. As I exited my room again, to go in search of Captain Nemo, I was abruptly confronted by Emily's tail—or, to be strictly accurate, her fluke. It was wagging, like a dog's caudal appendage, as Jenny carried her among the corridor, presumably aiming for something akin to an aquarium.

Emily smiled at me. She was beautiful, as she'd been designed to be, by myth and science alike.

"Still paradise," Jenny recited, making a jokey ritual of it.

"The Garden of Eden," I replied. But who, I wondered, was

the serpent?

"Except that there are no other merfolk here, as yet," Jenny added, pausing, as anyone might have done, having bumped into a friend while not in a particular hurry. "Maybe that's not such a bad thing, in the short term. I'd like Emily to myself for a little while longer, even if she will need to live with her own people eventually."

"I can understand that," I said. "Speaking as a man who talks more fondly to Venus fly-traps than to other human beings."

Emily looked me in the eyes, and then darted a rapid sideways glance over my shoulder. Nemo and Evangeline were coming along the corridor together. I wondered if it was what I'd muttered after removing the headset that had stirred them to action, or whether they were simply concerned because I'd removed it again. I was fairly sure that Xeno hadn't been able to overhear Oberon's part of the conversation—but what he'd heard of mine must have been worrying enough.

"I couldn't get through to Napoleon," I said to Nemo, blandly. "The set's dead."

He frowned, but didn't accuse me of lying. "That's unfortunate," he said, biting his plastic lip. "If it's a malfunction, we ought to be able to repair it." He held out his hand.

"I don't think it is," I said, folding up the set again and returning it to my pocket. "I think it's sabotage. Napoleon might be in trouble. Have you got some other communication system that can put me in touch with him?"

"Of course. You'd better use the equipment in the main station—it's carefully shielded and shouldn't be vulnerable to any kind of subtle sabotage. It's just a short walk up the hill." He moved off immediately, hardly having glanced at Jenny. Evangeline had to take on the task of paying due homage to Emily.

"Is it possible," I asked Nemo, as I fell into step with him, "that Oberon has some kind of presence here—that he's known about your existence for a long time?"

Nemo frowned. "It's not impossible," he admitted. It probably wouldn't have mattered if he'd offered a different assessment, I thought. Oberon didn't seem to be intimidated by the impossible.

When we were safely outside, well out of earshot of Jenny Haniver—who had gone on her way, freeing Evangeline to hurry after us—I said: "By the way, what kind of intelligence did Xeno build into Emily's brain? Did he engineer the Asperger transfiguration, inhibit it or leave the matter to chance? Or did he have some other notion of the sort of neuroarchitectural equipment that a mermaid might need?"

"I don't believe he made any specific modification of the brain," Nemo said. "The whole point was to produce a truly human being, albeit with a dolphin's hind-quarters."

"Of course," I said. "But it's no longer easy, is it, to say what we might mean by a *truly* human being? We all think of ourselves as true humans...perhaps even Xeno...but if what you want me to put to Napoleon is the human viewpoint that he might otherwise be without, then Xeno must think that some of us are truer humans than others, mustn't he? Is the rumor true that the reason Hemans' research ran into so much hostility was that his experimental subjects turned out to be smarter than their models...truer humans that Mother Nature's model?"

"Smarter isn't necessarily truer," Evangeline put in. She had caught us up, and heard most of my little speech.

I turned to look at her, and then turned back to Nemo. "Are the swine-bred subject to the Asperger transfiguration?" I asked. "Naturally, that is?"

"No more and no less so than the human-bred," he replied, "so far as we can tell. Our sample isn't very large. In any case, that probably isn't the only variant neurological disposition to which humans are naturally subject—as we'd know full well, if the Spasm hadn't interrupted research."

There was a hint of anxiety in his eyes. I wondered what trains of thought might be set in motion if anyone were to mention to Alexander Chesterton, without properly preparing the ground, that the St. Helenians were interested in mental engineering as well as physical engineering. But what could Jurgen Horowitz's recent discovery be, after all, but a specialized instance of applied homeotics? If the Commonwealth's politicians hadn't given much thought to the wider possibilities of the technology as yet, they would certainly begin to do so very soon—and if they were starting from its application to mental engineering rather than physical engineering....

"If Napoleon had wanted to contact me earlier today," I said, thinking aloud rather than merely putting the point to Nemo, "he could have done so...even if the set was dead, all he'd have had to do was let you know. He's doing everything he can to leave me out of this—so why should I insist on thrusting myself back in?"

"He's trying to protect you," Nemo said, stating the obvious. He was quick to follow up, though, with more telling points. "Do you really want to be protected? Do you really want to be left out? He might have your best interests at heart, but does he really know what they are? Isn't it up to you to decide what they are?"

"But you don't have my best interests—or his—at heart," I pointed out. "You want me to talk to him for your own reasons."

"Absolutely. We believe, though, that our interests and his coincide—and we're hoping that you'll see things the same way. Frankly, we're hoping that you can help to persuade Napoleon to let *you* act as a go-between in a three-way negotiation. We don't say that it won't be dangerous for you to expose your in that sort of situation, but in our estimation, you're the only one who can possibly play the role."

"The three parties in question being Napoleon, Xeno, and the Commonwealth? I'm not sure that the Commonwealth are going to like that—a man they've always suspected to be a covert enemy of the state mediating negotiations with two rogue silvers, as if each AI were on a par with the entire human race."

"On the contrary—Chesterton's bosses were the ones who tried to set it up that way in the first place. When they wanted to make advances to Napoleon, they elected to do it through you.

Our involvement has complicated the situation, but we think they'll stick to their original plan. They're still procrastinating over our direct overtures, apparently feeling that they'd rather deal with one rogue at a time, and having already made their choice. At present, they're talking to Napoleon directly, but we think they'd still prefer you to serve as Napoleon's mouthpiece, in order to keep him one step removed, and we hope that they'll jump at the chance to work that way, even if it means taking us aboard along with you. In fact, they might well prefer it. As for being an enemy of the state, they know perfectly well that you aren't—that you're as close to being genuinely independent as anyone they have, potentially able to win the trust and support of Sarah Valk's contingent. Fate might have thrust this upon you unexpectedly, Dr. Maclaine, but the simple fact is that you're currently the likeliest person there is to be able to anchor this whole process, and improve everyone's chances of a satisfactory outcome. Napoleon might not want to put that weight on your shoulders, but he really won't have any alternative, if you volunteer formally."

"And some have greatness thrust upon them," I muttered. No wonder Oberon had decided to make direct contact with me... but had he done so in order to pour poison in my ear, or to tip me off about Xeno's true intentions? Liar or not, one thing he'd said was beyond doubt: I was going to have to make up my own mind.

"Napoleon doesn't have to play it that way," I added. "If he insists on keeping me out of it, he can—simply be dropping out himself."

"He won't," said Nemo, confidently. "He's committed now. Anyway, if you insist, he can't say no. You're Cade Carlyle Maclaine. You may be the copy rather than the original, but you're still in a privileged position. Xeno doesn't have anyone comparable, and neither does Oberon."

"And what if I don't want to act as your mouthpiece as well as his? What if I decide that I'm *not* on your side?"

"But you *are* on our side," said Captain Nemo—or Xeno,

speaking through the cyborg—"or will be, once you've thought it through."

"From a human viewpoint," I added, a trifle sarcastically.

"Exactly," said Nemo, seemingly satisfied. I couldn't quite follow his logic—but he was the servant of the expert in convolution, the master of paradoxes and island paradises. The one thing I was fairly certain that the cyborg didn't any longer have, though, and probably wouldn't ever understand again, was a human viewpoint...especially if he thought of himself as a *true* human, and the rest of us as defective models spoiled by Mother Nature.

If I'd been talking to Alexander Chesterton I could have said, with a perfectly clear conscience: "Give me one good reason why I should help you." I wasn't, though; I was talking to an independent AI, who thought he already had.

The hill—which was, in fact, much more of a mountain-side than anything that would have been called a hill in Scotland—proved far more exhausting than Nemo's mention of "a short walk" had suggested, and it seemed to me that we were almost on top of the peak before they ushered me into the installation where I could supposedly be put in secure radio contact with Napoleon. I presumed that its situation had been chosen as much for symbolic reasons as practical ones. There was an armored shack full of equipment there—an odd jumble of the archaic and the modern—with a broad window overlooking the wooded slopes, the town, the harbor and the sea. A section of the window was open, to let in a breeze that was a little too stiff to be merely cooling; perhaps "bracing" would be the most apt adjective. I didn't mind the breeze at all, though; I wanted to keep my wits sharp.

"Carly?" Napoleon said, as soon as the channel was open. "The headset went off-line. I've been trying to find a way to contact you. Are you all right?"

"Safe and well," I assured him. "How are things at your end?"

"Not good," he said. "Your disappearance, along with the mother and the mermaid, caused quite a stir, and your sudden reappearance on the scene, seemingly as Xeno's pawn, has cast a definite shadow over my attempts to strike up a meaningful dialogue with Alexander Chesterton. All sorts of conspiracy theories appear to buzzing round. Oddly enough, though, Chesterton seems to be on your side. He's trying to convince his superiors that you aren't one of Xeno's agents."

"But I am, whether I like it or not," I told him, grimly. "Is that going to spoil things with Chesterton's masters?"

"I hope not," he said, "but it really would be best if you could stay out of it and let me handle it. Maybe the headset going dead is a blessing. I can talk to Xeno as well as Chesterton; I'm the only one that stands a chance of setting up some kind of agreement."

"Xeno doesn't think so," I said, reluctantly playing my part. "According to Nemo, Chesterton doesn't think so either. Xeno wants me involved. Are you in contact with any of the other rogues?—Oberon, for instance?"

"He's made overtures. If necessary, I can bring him to the table. In the short term, though, I'd rather not. The only way we're going to get anywhere is one step at a time. Xeno's already made it impossible to keep him out, but none of the others has brought anything to the table as yet. For now, the key question is the status of St. Helena, and its relationship to the Commonwealth. If we can settle that, at least on a temporary basis, that will automatically confer a legal status on Xeno... and, potentially, on the other free silvers, me included."

"I honestly think that you might have to let me help," I said. "Chesterton doesn't like or trust me, any more than he likes or trusts you, but he must think that he can route some sort of a deal through me, or I'd never have been dragged into this mess in the first place. Everybody wants a deal of some sort, don't they? Nobody really wants an orgy of violence. Even if St. Helena didn't have a sub full of nuclear warheads and you didn't have a ring of armed satellites at your disposal, the Masters of the Commonwealth wouldn't actually *want* to blast all hell out of St. Helena, would they? What everybody actually wants, at the end of the day, is a quiet life. Nobody wants their own para-noia to run riot, let alone anyone else's."

"They're frightened, Carly," Napoleon said. "They're fright-ened of me, of Xeno, of the other free silvers…and now they're frightened of Hemans' mock-humans too. And how can I blame them, when I'm frightened too?"

"So am I," I admitted. "They're frightened of me, too, because of the influence I have over you…but I have a better chance of soothing their fear than you do, simply because I'm only human. That's why I need to talk to Chesterton—not on my behalf but yours, and Xeno's too…and maybe others."

"I can see the logic of the strategy," Napoleon conceded. "Has Xeno made any threat against you, in the event that I refuse to cooperate?"

"No—he's being very careful. Kid gloves all the way, since the abduction itself—and he's even tried to pass that off as an accident. He hasn't even attempted to bribe me, much. All I've been asked to do is lend you a human viewpoint, and think hard about Emily Haniver's true significance. I have to confess that I don't know what that really means, or what Xeno expects me to conclude."

"Nor do I—but you might as well play the game. What *do* you think the mermaid's significance is?"

"Mythological mermaids were supposed to be seductresses—sirens whose song tempted sailors to their doom—but I don't think that's the way he expects me to think. From *my* view-point, as a xenogeneticist, she's triumph of the art, as striking a demonstration of the potential of applied homeotics as any clever pig in human form, if not even more striking…and, in consequence, a symbol of infinite golden opportunity…but I'm hardly possessed of a typical human viewpoint, am I?"

"Why not?"

"The simple fact that I'm a xenogeneticist would probably put paid to that.…but even if I weren't, I'm a clone of Cade Carlyle Maclaine. What chance did I ever have of being typical, or if living a typical life?"

"Who does, in today's world...or any other?"

I was tempted to answer: *almost everybody*, but I knew that it wouldn't be true. He and I had been living in interesting times all our lives, and so had our makers and parents, and our makers' parents, no matter how their parenthood had been contrived. "Normality" was a nostalgic pipe-dream of the masters of the Commonwealth. There was no normal life to be lived, any longer, and the only reason why anyone had ever thought that such a thing had existed, before the Crash, was that it was easer then for people to bury their heads in the sand and pretend that the world wasn't changing, even though it never paused in its evolution for an hour or a year, let alone a lifetime. Even at the very best of times—or the very worst, depending on your point of view—the only people who had ever been able to deny that change was going on, fatally corrosive of any and all attempts to stabilize the world and establish an enduring normality, were people with no imagination. And that was something else that mermaids, even fake ones, represented: the relentlessness of the human imagination in seeing beyond mere existence, in being able to reach into realms of possibility...and beyond, into realms of absurdity and paradox. Except that mermaids were no longer absurd and paradoxical. They had been decisively and dramatically translocated into the realm of the possible.

"Who does?" I agreed. "And yet we try. We keep our heads down, feigning inertia even when we're secretly not inert—humans and AIs alike. We all cling to the status quo, because we're all reluctant to let it go, afraid of what might replace it. But circumstances move on. Even Mother Nature, it seems—old Gaia herself—admits that when things get tough, reckless innovation and flexibility are essential. Maybe Cade would have been glad to discover that his Trojan Cockroach plan was just one more duplication of something Nature had already devised, and that life on Earth didn't need the provocation of orbital omnispore-banks to overcome obstacles to evolution. And even if he wouldn't...there's no reason why I can't."

"Time is of the essence, Dr. Maclaine," Evangeline whispered in my ear. "We don't have enough to spare for this sort of digression."

"You need to put me through to Alexander Chesterton now," I said to Napoleon. "And you have to give me your blessing to act of your behalf. I know it's hard, but if we don't do this, who will? If we can't, who can? Trouble's arrived—we have to try to sort it out."

He could have said no. He could have told me not to be ridiculous—that if he couldn't sort out out, I had no chance. He didn't. He didn't say anything at all, for a moment or two. Then he said: "Chesterton's agreeable. He wants to fix up a face-to-face meeting, and his people are willing to send a delegation to St. Helena, in the circumstances. That's good, I think. Xeno's agreeable too."

I turned briefly to glance at Nemo. He simply nodded. Xeno was, I assumed, more than agreeable.

"I'll step aside," Napoleon told me. "You can take it from here, Carly. It's what Cade would have wanted, I think. He might have been paranoid, but his heart was always in the right place." It seemed a very strange thing for an outlaw AI without a heart to say, but I wasn't surprised to hear him say it. If he'd had a heart, it would have been in the right place.

No sooner had he said it, though, than the radio connection went stone dead.

CHAPTER SIXTEEN

I WAITED FOR A SECOND or two, in case the silence was just a pause before Alexander Chesterton came through, but I had an awful suspicion that it wasn't. I looked at the cyborg again, and said: "Not impossible after all, then."

"Shit," said Nemo. For once, he presumably wasn't speaking as Xeno, who had no bowel.

"What now?" I asked.

"I don't know," he replied, "but if I'm right in judging what *that* means, we'd best get out of here."

He nodded his head toward the open window. It was a big window, and my poor humans eyes didn't pick up what he meant immediately, but by dint of peering hard, I was eventually able to make out a little black dot in the azure expanse. It might have been an albatross, if albatrosses had survived the Spasm, but they hadn't, and it wasn't. Its apparent size wasn't just an illusion of distance, though; it really wasn't much bigger than an albatross, and it was gliding much as an albatross just have glided, in order to save energy and fly for vast distances without using overmuch fuel. It had fuel, though; it was simply preserving it for more aggressive purposes.

We had plenty of time to get out of the shack before the drone opened fire, and blasted the place to smithereens with a single shot, armor and all. If its sender had only been trying to prove a point, it could have turned away then, and soared serenely onwards, but it didn't. It began to turn in a tight arc, and to lose elevation. Apparently, it had another target programmed in.

"Shit," I said, in my turn. "Emily."

I didn't know that Emily was the second target of course, any more than I knew whether it was Oberon who was trying to upset the apple-cart, or whether the Commonwealth's hardliners had decided that shooting first as a better idea than sending a delegation of their weaker-kneed peers to St. Helena for face-to-face talks with a motley crew of renegades. I was just afraid that she might be. She was, after all, the device that Xeno had used to make his point. Whether Alexander Chesterton's rivals had sent the drone, or Oberon, it was now making a point of its own.

I was already running down the slope, and so were Nemo and Evangeline—but Nemo's cyborg body had lost in elasticity what it had gained in durability. He was no superman when it came to athletics. Evangeline and I outdistanced him easily, and we continued to head in the same direction, without either of us taking an evident lead. I tried to keep my eyes on the drone while I ran, trying not to let it cross my kind that it *might* be after me.

If it *was* after me, it didn't get to me. It never fired a second missile. St. Helena's defenses had been taken by surprise, but they were by no means impotent. Long before I reached the town, even travelling downhill at something close to full tilt, the drone exploded in mid-air, shot down by a bullet as deadly as its own.

The war that nobody wanted had started; the question was no longer whether it could be prevented but whether it could be stopped—and if so, how.

Once the drone had been neutralized, Evangeline broke silence: "Head straight for the *Nautilus*, Dr. Maclaine," she said. "I'll collect Jenny and Emily." Her tone implied that it was an invitation rather than a command, but it didn't really matter. If more drones were going to follow the first—and the mere possibility was threat enough—the sub was probably the safest place to be. I still didn't know for sure whether it was armed or not, but even if the only thing it could do was hide, that seemed a useful option to have, at present.

Evangeline seemed to be expecting some sort of reply, so I nodded. We were already on the outskirts of town, having come down the mountain considerably faster than we'd gone up, and she veered left toward the hotel. I headed straight for the harbor—or as straight as I could, given the awkward topography. I was still running at a good pace, in spite of the fact that my legs were aching and I was developing a stitch in my side, so I was thrown completely off balance when something cannoned into me from the side and knocked me over.

It was a bad fall, and it jarred me horribly as well as expelling the air from my lungs. I put out my arms to absorb some of the shock, but bashed both my elbows against unforgiving stone, and my knees also collided with the hard ground. I'd shut my eyes reflexively, and they filled up with tears when I tried to force them open again, so I saw hardly anything of what was happening before the sunlight was abruptly cut off and I was plunged into darkness. I knew, though, that I'd been grabbed—probably by at least two people.

I tried to put up a fight, even though my elbows were hurting so badly that my arms seemed to be nothing but sheaves of pain. I had no chance. I'd probably have accomplished more by screaming for help, but I didn't seem to have breath enough to whimper.

"Stop struggling, you idiot," a male voice hissed in my ear. "We're trying to save your life!"

I was bundled down a flight of steps. I knew better that to take what the voice had said at face value, but I stopped struggling anyway, because I knew that it wasn't doing any good and I was in enough pain already. I lost track of time, but it couldn't have been more than a matter of seconds—maybe half a minute at the most—before I was dumped into an armchair. The room, which I assumed to be a cellar, wasn't completely dark, but it didn't seem to have any windows, and the lamp burning in a corner—literally burning, because it was some kind of oil lamp—was hooded.

I heard the sound of a door being shut and locked before

the hood was released, and I saw a vaguely human silhouette looming over me. It was burly, but I couldn't make out much else, except for a shock of unruly, and presumably dark-colored, hair.

"Sorry about that, sir," said the male voice. "No time."

Then he reached down. I flinched reflexively, fearing further injury, but all he did was fit a headset to my skull, presumably similar in all its essential features to the one in my pocket.

"Don't be alarmed, Dr. Maclaine," said a different voice, in my ear. "We really are attempting to save your life."

I was still in sufficient pain to wonder whether I might be dying, but reason told me that it was only a matter of cuts and bruises. Even so, the request not to be alarmed seemed a bit rich.

"Oberon?" I said.

"Believe me, Dr. Maclaine," the voice said. "That last place you want to be, at this moment, is aboard the *Nautilus*. It's not going to be easy reining the Commonwealth hardliners in—but my first priority, right now, has to be neutralizing the sub. I'm putting you through to Napoleon now."

"Carly?" said yet another voice. "Are you all right?"

"No!" I snapped. "What the hell is going on?"

"Chesterton was stabbed in the back. He and his people were willing to deal—but that very willingness split the Masters. Their alliance has been brittle for years. Chesterton's party have the bulk of the security forces, but we're on the brink of civil war. They moved against me, too, and Xeno—but I had my escape-route planned and ready, and Xeno seems to be ready and willing to strike back. Oberon's trying to prevent that...or says that he is. Frankly, I don't know whether he's on the side of the angels or not, but he's right about one thing: if he really can take out the *Nautilus*, you don't want to be aboard it."

I wasn't even sure what side the angels were on. All I could think of to say was: "What about Emily?"

There was no reply to that, presumably because the next voice to come on line was Alexander Chesterton's. "That was *not* my doing, Maclaine," he said. "You have to believe that. We were so scared of a double-cross by the AIs that we took our eye off our own people. We'll contain it, if we can. We *will* contain it. Trust me on that. If you have any influence with the AIs at all, you *have* to stop them shooting back. Do you understand me? Promise them amnesty, citizenship, sovereignty…any damn thing you like. Just *stop them shooting back!*"

The negotiations, I realized, had already started. He'd wanted us to sit down round a conference table, like civilized people—just as he'd carefully sat me down with Sarah Valk and introduced me to Jenny Haniver, because that was the way he and his bureaucratic kind did things—but it was too late for that now. We had to improvise whatever compromise we could, from where we now stood. The only problem—apart from the fact that my elbows were still giving me gyp—was that I really didn't know whether I had any influence at all over anyone, let alone the authority to stop them shooting back.

"Tell him that I won't shoot, for now," said Napoleon.

"And tell him that I won't either," said Oberon. "Tell him to concentrate all his own efforts on disrupting Xeno's traffic. I'll take care of the sub, but God only knows what else he has up his sleeve."

"Can you hear me?" Alexander Chesterton screamed. "Answer me, damn it!" Evidently, he couldn't hear them.

I was glad, in a way, that I had no time to think. I would only have lost myself in a labyrinth of possibilities based on the liar's paradox—because I had no way of knowing, at the end of the day, whether any of them was telling the truth, or which one it might be. I had no alternative but to follow my gut.

"I can hear you, Mr. Chesterton," I said. "Just concentrate your own efforts on reining in your own renegades, and leave the AIs to me. If you can put your own house in order, there's a chance we can do likewise. Will you do that?"

"I'm already doing it," Chesterton replied.

"That and *only* that," I insisted. "Lay off the free silvers—*all of them*. Leave them to me. Okay?"

"Okay," he said. "Promise them anything…but for God's

sake, don't let me down."

"I won't," I said. Promise them anything, he'd said. It was the only way to go.

"Napoleon?" I said then. "Can you hear me?"

"Yes."

"Oberon?"

"Yes."

"You have to bring in Xeno too."

"That's not…," Oberon began.

"Just do it," I said.

There as a moment's hesitation, but then a new voice chimed in: "Dr. Maclaine? Where are you?"

"Never mind that," I said. "I don't know whether there's any way out of this mess, but I can think of one thing that might be worth trying. If it's going to work, though, you all have to agree. You have to disarm. I don't even know if any of you actually possess the deterrents that everybody's so shit scared of, but if you do, you have to get rid of them *now*. Napoleon, you have to blow up the Chaos Patrol, if you can—or hand control of the satellites over to Chesterton if you can't. Xeno, you have to surrender or scuttle the *Nautilus*. Oberon, you have to make whatever show you can of disposing of whatever weapons you've got. If you won't do that, we're all doomed—this will escalate, and nothing will stop it. Will you do it?"

In a better world, perhaps more human and perhaps less, it might even have worked. It might have qualified as a stroke of luck, if not a stroke of genius. We weren't in that world, though. They all hesitated, for a second or two, each one waiting for the other two to speak, but when one of them finally did, the snowball melted, and hell was given free rein.

"No," said Xeno. Maybe he really did want to take over the world, or maybe he was just scared.

"No," said Napoleon, as if the reaction were purely automatic.

I didn't wait for Oberon, whose reply was now irrelevant. "In that case," I said, "Oberon: take out the sub—*and then stop*. Napoleon: whatever happens, *hold your fire*. Xeno: if Oberon really can take out the sub, be ready to admit defeat, and *don't do anything else as stupid as what you just did."*

Then I looked up at the hairy man who had intercepted me on my way to the Nautilus and taken me prisoner for my own good. "I'd have said the same, you know, if I'd actually been aboard the sub. Even if taking it out meant taking me out too…because I'm crazy that way."

He shrugged his shoulders. He hadn't a clue what was going on. He was only following orders.

Xeno's men broke the cellar door down then, having obviously figured out, one way or another, where I was. It couldn't have been a difficult problem, given that I'd been snatched off the street within sight of the harbour, in broad tropical daylight. In their minds, they were undoubtedly attempting yet another "rescue"—but they were too late. The die was cast.

It only remained to see whether the free silvers would follow my second set of orders-cum-suggestions, or not, and whether there was still some slight chance of saving the Second Renaissance from going the same way as the first.

CHAPTER SEVENTEEN

EVANGELINE SEEMED TO be in charge of the rescue party. In fact, the more I saw of Evangeline, the more she seemed to be in charge of all sorts of things.

"Are you all right, Dr. Maclaine?" she asked, when I staggered out into the sunlight again, having been dragged back up the stairs in a rather unceremonious manner. I checked out my arms and legs, now that there was light enough to permit a proper inspection. There didn't seem to be very much blood staining my shirt and trousers—my surskin was already hard at work sealing off the damaged tissue and anesthetizing the pain—and nothing seemed to be broken or sprained, so I replied in the affirmative.

"Is there time to stop the *Nautilus* putting out to sea?" I demanded, without pause.

She replied by extending an arm and a pointing finger. I followed its direction, shading my eyes from the setting sun with my hand.

The submarine was already outside the harbor, but not yet far enough from shore to dive. Captain Nemo was still visible on the conning tower, looking back over his shoulder at the shore. He could probably have picked me out if I'd waved.

I looked up at the sky, scanning it anxiously for drones, or any other kind of aircraft.

Evangeline was scanning too. "Nothing," she said, perhaps more out of optimism than conviction, but with a distinct note of self-satisfaction in her voice. "Unless a laser beam's going to plummet down from orbit, he's safe." By *he* she presumably meant Nemo.

"Is Emily aboard?" I asked.

"Yes," she said. "Emily and other key assets. We need to be sure that they're safe, and we can't be certain that we can defend the island successfully without sustaining heavy losses. Our best chance of preserving it is to keep our deterrent intact. If *anyone* launches a further assault against us, we *will* hit back." She obviously figured that Oberon was still listening in over the apparatus that his minion had placed on my head. It was silent, for the moment, but I wasn't prepared to assume that it was dead. I had a suspicion that *everyone* was listening in, agog to se what would happen next, and that the hush was pregnant with alarm.

Because the headset had been put on by someone else, in poor light, I didn't know whether the mouthpiece was rigged out with a camera, and squinting in that direction didn't settle the question. I decided that it didn't much matter. Even if I wasn't functioning as a long-distance eye, there would be eyes around… and one way or another, what they saw would reach Oberon's rapt attention, and Napoleon's, and Alexander Chesterton's, as well as Xeno's.

I still wasn't in a waving mood, but Evangeline was. She raised her arm in a kind of salute. Nemo might have been waiting for the signal, or it might just have been well-timed. He returned the gesture, and then shouted something at the crew members down below. Within another half-minute, I figured, he would have sealed the hatch and prepared the vessel to dive.

"You have to stop him," I said to Evangeline, convinced that she could, if she wanted to.

"I can't," she said—meaning that she wouldn't. She really did think that he best chance of securing St. Helena's future was to preserve the island's nuclear deterrent—or its alleged nuclear deterrent. There was no way I could convince her otherwise… certainly not in the space of half a minute.

Nemo didn't get the time he needed, though. He didn't seem

to be in any particular hurry, but it wouldn't have mattered if he had made all possible haste. The sky was still crystal clear, turning a lovely shade of cobalt blue as the reddening sun descended gracefully toward the western waves. There were no aircraft or missiles this side of the horizon, and not the slightest hint of anything plunging from beyond the atmosphere—but from a distance, I could see what Nemo hadn't yet noticed.

The sea in front of the submarine's course had begun to seethe like a cauldron.

I watched it seethe, puzzled and fascinated. I still hadn't worked out what it might be when the cables started shooting up from beneath the surface and wrapping themselves around the vessel's hull, already tilting it sideways.

Nemo took notice then, but it was far too late for him to get the hatch shut, and he didn't even try. He didn't know what was happening ether, and was still trying to figure it out.

Then the carapace briefly broke the surface, and I guessed. I wasn't the only one. Nemo must have guessed too. The people who had pulled me out of the cellar where I'd be momentarily held had paused along with their leader; Evangeline and I were at the heart of a crowd, all of whose members knew why Captain Nemo had chosen his pseudonym, and what the name *Nautilus* signified…and they guessed too.

Everyone who could see had guessed, and everyone who had guessed gasped, as if in stupefied chorus. Nobody could believe it, but everybody could *see* it, and they all knew that their eyes didn't lie.

The apparent cables weren't cables: they were tentacles. The *Nautilus* was under attack from a giant cephalopod.

The *Nautilus* was a compact vessel, but it wasn't tiny. It was bigger than any other vessel in Jamestown's harbour, including the cargo ship tethered to the quay. It had to be heavy, in spite of its buoyancy. I knew that it was armed, presumably with something more than inter-continental ballistic missiles—but none of that mattered, in the context of its present situation. I couldn't measure the monster exactly, but it was bigger than the sub, and far more massive. Each of its many tapering tentacles was hundreds of meters long, and its carapace must have been at least twice as voluminous as the submarine's hull

I didn't know exactly what the cephalopod was, although I presumed that it must be kin to one of the species that had been thought extinct until recently, but it didn't really matter whether it was a giant squid or an inflated cuttlefish with delusions of grandeur, or some kind of xenoplastic patchwork; the point was that it was a true giant—probably the largest organism in the world.

Evangeline swore violently.

The impossible we do at once, I thought, *the miraculous sometimes takes a little longer.* Napoleon and Alexander Chesterton had been correct in their suspicions. There had been secret stations by the sea—or perhaps under it—during the Plague War, and their records of overt and covert experimentation in marine biology hadn't been lost. Napoleon didn't have them, but Oberon did...and for decades, perhaps for centuries, Oberon had been continuing the work, by whatever means he could improvise. Maybe his primary objective had merely been to assist Mother Nature with the repopulation and revitalization of marine environments. Maybe his driving purpose had been to armor himself, as best he could, against the weapons his peers and potential enemies possessed. Maybe he'd simply read Jules Verne, and figured that every *Nautilus* deserves to fight its classic battle...except that, if I was remembering correctly, the valiant crew of Verne's *Nautilus*, armed only with whaling harpoons and a couple of small guns, had won.

The crew of St. Helena's *Nautilus* had no chance.

One of the lashing tentacles wound around the cyborg Captain Nemo, and lifted him high into the air. The others continued to roll the ship over, letting water flow into the hatch that Nemo hadn't managed to close in time.

The battle could have been over in a matter of seconds, without a shot being fired—but it wasn't. The monstrous cephalopod—or whoever was controlling it—hesitated, not out of uncertainty but purposively. It could have squeezed the life out of the cyborg, or hurled him through the air to smash against the harbor wall, but in fact it gave him time and space to draw some kind of side-arm and start shooting.

I couldn't blame Nemo for that—he must, after all, have been in something of a panic. He did take aim, though, at the cephalopod's huge eyes, each one of which was five or ten times the size of a human head. Some of the bullets probably missed, but not all. The monster took the shots, and soaked them up.

I could see people in the water, evidently coming out of the hatch through which the water was still flowing—*flowing*, not flooding. The monster was actually *letting* them out…and as it began to pluck they out of the water, one by one, it still didn't squeeze them or smash them. Instead, it held them out of the water, in mid-air, making certain that they could breathe. It even did the same for the baby mermaid, who surely wouldn't have been able to swim in the seething water.

The creature could have dived immediately, taking the sub and all its personnel down in one fell swoop, but instead, it set about trying to save the lives of the vessel's crew and the island's "key assets." Maybe it didn't get them all, but it wasn't for lack of trying.

People were running along the harbor wall now, armed with rifles and heavier weapons that might have been built to launch rocket-propelled grenades.

"Stop them!" I said, sharply, to Evangeline. "They can't save the *Nautilus*—but they might kill the people the cephalopod's trying to save."

"Save!" she repeated, helplessly. If she had a radio or a phone on her person she didn't try to use it—but it didn't matter, because the people with the weapons had eyes and brains, and the logic of the situation was all-too-obvious by now. The people on the wall didn't open fire. They could see perfectly well that the squid, if it was a squid, was tempering aggression with mercy.

"Is something happening, Maclaine?" asked Alexander

Chesterton, his voice sharp enough to sting my unwary ears. He obviously knew that something was, but he didn't know what. As yet, he had no eyes on St. Helena. Any that I was wearing were obviously being hogged by Oberon.

"Yes it is, Mr. Chesterton," I said. "Just sit tight. Trust me. I told you I could handle the silvers, and I can. Just look after your own side of the deal, and wait. Everything is under control."

All free agents are liars. Sometimes you have to lie, and live in hope that time and tide will back you up.

Maybe a cynic would have suggested that the cephalopod, or its controller, might be using the crew and the mermaid as a human shield against the gunmen on the harbor wall, but the cynic would have been overstepping his warrant absurdly. The cephalopod didn't need a human shield. Nothing on Earth could have stopped it, now, from dragging the submarine down to wherever it wanted to take it—which, considering the sheerness of the slopes of the underwater volcano whose tip St. Helena was, might be a very long way down. And the only thing on Earth that could prevent the crew and passengers from going down after the ship, dragged down in the turbulent water that its sinking would leave behind, was the monster itself.

Which was exactly what the monster did. First, it towed the submarine back toward the shore, in order that its multitudinous tentacles—which numbered far more than eight, although I couldn't make an exact count, presumably disqualifying it from being considered an octopus, whatever its genomic ancestry might have been—could begin to set their human cargo down on the harbor wall.

What would have happened if anyone had opened fire at that point, I don't know—but nobody did. The people with the rifles and grenade-launchers laid them down, and reached out with their arms to accept Emily Haniver, Jenny, Captain Nemo, Kurt and a dozen others, all of who still seemed to be alive and kicking.

Afterwards, I suppose, the people on the harbor wall could have picked up their guns again and launched a salvo—a futile salvo, I assumed, but a gesture of defiance at the very least. They didn't. Nobody had negotiated anything, but a tacit bargain of sorts had been struck, which everyone present appeared to recognize. Perhaps the gunmen even realized that the squid was on a suicide mission, unlikely to survive the long, long journey up to the surface from the pressurized depths for much longer than was required to carry out its complex task, and that they didn't need to make any further contribution to its eventual demise.

At any rate, the crowd simply watched as the monster moved away again, leaking huge drops of liquid from its eyes, which presumably weren't tears but might as well have been. It took the hopefully-empty *Nautilus* with it. When the squid slowly submerged again, only a few hundred meters from the shore, everyone watching from the island knew that the submarine would never be seen again by human eyes, and that it no longer mattered whether any nuclear warheads that it was carrying might have been viable or not.

Oberon had said that he could take out the sub. Oberon had taken out the sub—in such a way that the game was still in play, and hell hadn't yet broken loose.

I knew that there had to have been numerous cameras on what had just happened, even though there were no surrogate eyes through which Alexander Chesterton had been able to see what was going on as it actually happened. It all had to be digitized, preserved for posterity. Maybe it hadn't been broadcast yet; maybe neither Alexander Chesterton nor Napoleon had a clue as to what had happened yet—but the news would spread, sooner rather than later. I didn't have to say a word.

"We were penetrated," Evangeline murmured, bitterly. "From the very beginning. Oberon's been in our midst since the first wave of immigrants. We never had the monopoly on applied homeotics."

"*That* wasn't a product of applied homeotics," I said. I couldn't be absolutely sure, but I felt that I ought to claim the credit loudly, just in case. "You don't need applied homeotics to engineer invertebrates. *That* was a product of the Trojan Cephalopod Plan. *That* was Cade Carlyle Maclaine's invention, albeit applied by other hands than his...plus a little cunning cyborgization to put a quasi-human mind in parallel with its tiny native brain. The real Earthly Underworld has always been the ocean depths—if you can claim the kingship of that realm, you're untouchable."

It was bluster, of course. Oberon wasn't untouchable, Ninety-nine per cent of him, at least, had to be on land, as touchable as the core resources of any other AI, if they could be located... but the point was that the would-be King of the Underworld hadn't just shown his strength, but his restraint. He had made it plausible, with a graphic demonstration, that all he wanted was a quiet life, and that he was prepared to let others live quietly as well. He had even saved the baby mermaid.

With a little luck, I thought, the giant cyborg squid with the multitudinous tentacles might also have saved the world.

CHAPTER EIGHTEEN

THE LOSS OF THE submarine didn't make it any easier for the islanders to return me to the Isle of Wight, of course, and it might till have been convenient, in purely geographical terms, for Alexander Chesterton to bring Mahomet to the mountain— but by the time everybody had figured out that the apparent balance of power had shifted, there seemed to be good symbolic reasons for holding further negotiations in the bosom of the Commonwealth.

Once I had been returned, the scene moved fairly rapidly from Shanklin to London. England's capital was more a skeleton than a shadow of its former self, but it was already in the process of grabbing its former glory with greedy hands; the burgeoning city was already undisputed as the economic heart, not only of Phoenix England but the entire Commonwealth. As a Scot, I would naturally have preferred Paris, Rome, Barcelona, Jerusalem or almost anywhere else, but history maintains a certain momentum even through a catastrophe as devastating as the Spasm, and myths die hard. London had to be my stage.

It wasn't really *my* stage, of course; arguably, I wasn't even the leading man—but I was no pawn or spear-carrier. I was a player, now. I wasn't just Napoleon's man any more; I was the AIs' man. I'd assumed responsibility for acting as their go-between, and I was stuck with that responsibility. I was only one link in a tangled silver-studded chain, but I was a vital one. Logically speaking, I was entirely unnecessary, but in symbolic terms, I was indispensable. The free silvers had voices and minds of their own, but they didn't have bums to put on seats, or even faces to put on screens. Xeno had Nemo, of course, but even he needed me now.

Everybody knew by the time the London circus began to take form that it was Xeno who had wrecked the deal I'd originally offered—and that deal too acquired more symbolic value in having been turned down than it could probably have retained if it had been accepted. If Oberon had been right about Xeno and the swine-bred harboring megalomaniac ambitions, they had been forced to put them firmly aside and commit themselves to the thesis that the meek might, after all, inherit the Earth—and certainly deserved to do so. Nemo didn't have enough moral credit to take a conference seat all by himself. I did. At the universal moral credit bank, my account as well into the black, even if it did bear the name of Cade Carlyle Maclaine.

It could all have gone horribly wrong before I ever got back to England, of course, if Chesterton's Mahomet hadn't been able to get a grip on his own lunatic fringe, but that worked out too—apparently. For the time being, apparently was enough.

Napoleon didn't blow up the Chaos Patrol, but he did provide convincing evidence that the weapons built into a few of its satellites had been decommissioned. Was the evidence reliable? I don't know—but then, I didn't need to know. All I needed was the power to pretend. Oberon made gestures of the same sort, with respect to some potentially-nasty biological weapons, and so did Xeno. Nobody believed that any of them was toothless, but nobody any longer believed that they might bite like rabid dogs if looked at askance.

So, to cut a very long story short, the conference was convened in London, and slowly took shape, albeit in a rather amoebic fashion. All the interested parties sent delegates to the table, and the three titans of the Underworld weren't the only ones who availed themselves of my mediation. Ulysses and a dozen other free silvers made contact, including two who'd never come out of the closet before—and none was turned away, although I had to hire a whole ambassadorial staff to help me out.

AIs gifted with sentient autonomy didn't get citizenship, let alone sovereignty—at least not immediately—but they did get reassurances that allowed them to be convinced that the hunting season was well and truly over and that they were in no immediate danger of extermination, by the Commonwealth or by one anther. The citizens of the Commonwealth didn't get democracy either—at least, not immediately—but they got reassurances too, as to what the Architects of the Second Renaissance wouldn't attempt to do without at least attempting to observe the principle of informed consent.

Were the reassurances reliable? I don't know—but again, I didn't need to know. All I needed was grounds for hope, and a means of spinning things out.

The conference was big, and you know what even small committees are like…things can drag on forever, if you're not careful. Or, of course, if you are. Jaw-jaw is, as they say, better than war-war.

What I wanted most of all, of course, once I was back on English soil, was to get back to my plants. I needed to check that they were all right. I also needed to talk to them. It was by no means easy to find the time, now that I had other obligations, and every reason to spin them out, but the situation wasn't too bad, and I was in a position to make demands. Guildford was less than an hour's drive from London, unless the traffic was really bad, and even committees need to rest. I couldn't spend nearly as much time with my Venus fly-traps, Mimosas and porcupine-grasses as I wanted to, but I did what I could.

Nobody understood, of course, why I needed to do it—not even Sarah Valk, let alone Napoleon or Oberon. I wasn't her spokesman, of course—she had her own seat at the table and a bum to put on it—but she did regard me as a crucial ally, and she was just as avid for my attention as anyone else.

"Your personal research can wait, Carly," she told me, sternly. "It's the future of research in general that we have to guarantee."

"In order to look after the lawn," I replied, "we have to look after the individual blades of grass."

While I'd been away, my two girl-friends had found out about one another, so they'd probably have dumped me anyway, even if I'd capitulated with one or other of their ultimata, but when it became obvious that I'd far rather spend my limited time with the motile plants than with either of them, now that I hadn't got time for both or all three, they took umbrage.

"They can't talk back, you know," Paula told me. "They can't even hear you. And no matter how much raw meat you feed your giant Venus fly-traps, they're never going to pick up their roots and walk."

"Anything's possible," I assured her, mildly. "Even miracles. This is the world of the Second Renaissance. There are no biological limits. Even Mother Nature has cast off her shackles, at least for a while."

It was all to no avail. My love life went up in smoke.

There's absolutely no point in trying to summarize, let alone to detail, what went on at the conference sessions. Far too much was said, often at great length, and far too little came of it, in the early stages…except for the immensely valuable negatives. The world didn't end. Not many people died.

I'd like to say that none died, but a few did. There were a lot of resentments floating around the human world, and a good deal of fear. Even the giant squid, however manifestly heroic its actions had been, had sown as much fear as it had alleviated. Some people simply can't set aside the reflexive reactions of mythic horror. There were fights, brawls, riots and attempted assassinations—not many, but too many. With regard to the attempted assassinations, a few intended targets were hit, and considerably more innocent bystanders mown down in the cross-fire—as per usual. Did any of the targets deserve to die? Was there an arguable case that the world was better off without them? I don't know, but I can honestly say that I regretted them all.

Given my situation as the TV-advertised spokesman for the free silvers, I received far more than my fair share of death-threats, but I had good security. Alexander Chesterton still didn't like me, but he knew full well that I was now worth my weight in gold—and Napoleon was no longer the only covert operator who was determined to look after me. If I hadn't been an essentially modest person I might have begun to acquire a few delusions of grandeur myself. Even the sanest of people can go mad if he's on TV too frequently, and I had started out crazy...but I had a responsibility to rationality now, and I had to hold myself in check, using every method available to stay as sane as humanly possible

Occasionally, I called Jenny Haniver on the videophone, ostensibly to check up on Emily, but mainly because she was not only the sanest person I knew but the happiest.

"Still paradise," she said, every time.

"That's good," I told her on the tenth or eleventh occasion. "We're doing everything we can to keep it that way—especially Evangeline, who needs every last vestige of her diplomatic talent to plead for the swine-born. I'm helping as much as I can but I don't have enough fingers. She hates London—I think she's very homesick—but she's sticking it out. Hold Emily up so that I can get a good look at her."

"Isn't she growing?"

"Can she talk yet?"

"Don't be silly...give her time."

"I'm not being silly—just optimistic. She's cute now, but once she can talk, she'll be able to start playing her role for real."

"What role?"

"Her symbolic role, as a paradoxical but all-too-real example of a fusion of two worlds and an emblem of endless possibility. The world needs to fall in love with her, and everything she represents."

"How could anyone not love her? Although, as her mother, I suppose I'm the only one who's actually obliged."

"No, you're right. How could anyone not love her? It might take a little time, but it will work out for the best in the end."

"How are the mobile plants?"

"I'm doing my best, but I have to admit that progress has

stalled. Too many distractions. I spend as much time as I can with them, but they don't see enough of me, and they know it."

"You could get other people to talk to them."

"I know, but it wouldn't be the same."

"Why not? Why would they care. They can't hear you."

"I wish people wouldn't keep saying that. I've told you before—it all depends what you mean by *hear*. No, they don't have ears with eardrums and cochleas, or brains to decode the signals transmitted by such specialized sense-organs—but *Mimosa pudica* isn't called the sensitive plant for nothing. Sound is just movement—vibration in the air. The more my plants are able to move—and I'm using all my expertise to improve their abilities and their acceleration—the more reactive they become to movements round them. They're not *conscious* of their own responses to what I say to them, in the sense that you're conscious of what I'm saying to you, but that doesn't mean they're not affected by it, and it doesn't mean that they're not affected differently by different things I say, or by different voices. I might not the best person to judge whether or not I'm crazy, but I know full well that I'm not as crazy as some people think I am. Believe me, talking to my plants will some day bear fruit…if you'll forgive the pun."

"Was that a pun?" she asked, refusing to believe it. "Is that what you're actually trying to do? Nemo says that you're trying to develop new kinds of zoophytes…working towards plants that actually have the power of locomotion, or plants that can produce motile spores. Are you really trying to teach them to understand language, and talk back?"

"That might be a bit too ambitious," I admitted, "but sound is just movement. If plants can move, they can produce sounds, as well as reacting to sounds—and if their movement is to be organized, then orchestration is probably the best way to do it. You might think that it's not really communication, and I'd have difficulty persuading you otherwise by strictly rational means, but my plants and I really do have an understanding of sorts, and the more power of movement I can give them the better that understanding becomes." My new career as a diplomat was obviously loosening my tongue. I'd long grown used to keeping quiet about what I was really doing with my Mimosas and their friends, and what my medium-term objectives were—but Jenny was, after all, the mermaid's mother, and something of a symbol in her own right.

"You don't have to convince me of anything," she told me—which was true.

I went on anyway. "It all takes energy, of course—but plants can acquire energy readily enough, if they're carnivorous… provided, of course, they're an order of magnitude quicker than your average Venus fly-trap. I haven't succeeded yet in perfecting xemoplastic ubiquity between the *Dionaeas* and the *Mimosas*, because they're not as amenable to crossovers as the *Stirpas*, but innovative science is a slow business. Patience is the key—that and longevity. In time, with the aid of clever xenoplasty, and maybe a little applied homeotics…except that I don't really have the time any more. I've sold out. I'm a smiling, lying, loquacious diplomat nowadays, not a grim, obsessive, reclusive, painfully honest dyed-in-the-wool scientist. What would Cade think of me now, I wonder?"

"Spinning in his grave as we speak, I shouldn't wonder," she replied, refusing to supply the compliment I'd been fishing for.

"The dead are like the lilies of the field," I told her. "They toil not, neither do they spin."

"Not yet," she agreed. "But when you're eventually able to get back to work, who knows? There are no more biological limits, remember. I have the proof of that, wriggling in my arms."

I could have played the pedant and said that there might be hope for the lilies, toiling- and spinning-wise but not for the dead—but I didn't. As a true diplomat, I was generously prepared to let her have the last word. Anyway, how could I be sure?

CHAPTER NINETEEN

I WAS ADVISED several times that it was exceedingly unwise of me to travel so frequently between London and Guildford, especially at odd hours. I was also advised several times that the university was, by its very nature, an unsafe environment, with too large and heterogeneous a population. I was advised in no uncertain terms, more than once, that it was extremely unwise to insist on working in my lab alone, often at the dead of night, for hours at a stretch, all in the interests of "trying to teach my plants to dance." Somehow, that phrase of Nemo's had caught on, becoming an endless supply of jokes, especially in the media. That troubled my advisers too; they thought that I ought to move around as little as possible when the conference wasn't actually in season, and that whenever I did move, I should do so in secret.

"We can pick up on anything that's explicitly planned," Oberon assured me, "but there are always solitary and silent processes on why we can't spy. The Commonwealth's hardest hardliners probably have too much sense to hire hit-men, but down at the grass roots all kinds of resentments are swarming. There are people out there who sincerely believe that you're an enemy of the human race who's sold his soul to demons. You don't see them, because you've spent your life hanging out with scientists, but they're there. The Repopulation was more than a little reckless; it preserved far too much lunacy and idiocy, in the name of maximizing genetic diversity."

I didn't listen, and I was glad that I had sufficient authority to get my own way. One day, I knew, the ineffably tedious business of saving the world would be over…or, at least, safely handed over to other, more willing hands. Then, I wanted to be able to pick up my own life again. I wanted to be who I chose to be again, instead of the person cruel fate and unhappy coincidence had singled me out to be—and to do that, I needed to keep in touch with myself. I wasn't able to teach any more, because I wouldn't have been able to maintain a stable daytime timetable, but I could certainly spend time in my lab when I could generate a few spare hours.

I don't actually know how many potential troublemakers the official security forces stopped before I even caught sight of them, or them of me, or how many Napoleon and Oberon were able to intercept. Nor, obviously, can I tell what they might have done if they'd got through to me. The one who finally did must have been cunning, as well as completely crazy and self-contained, given that he evaded all the silvers' espionage, and he must have been more than a little lucky, to catch Alexander Chesterton's loyal but not-entirely-committed hirelings off-guard—but I have to admit that when he reached the last hurdle of all, I was the one who made the crucial blunder.

I was absorbed in what I was doing, and when I was in that frame of mind, it was as if I stepped back in time to balmier and more innocent days. When there was a knock on the door of my inner sanctum, I didn't think about it, even to make a semi-conscious assumption. I just took it for granted, quite obliviously, that it was someone coming to tell me that they loved me—even though the people who had once been in the habit of doing that no longer did. If it had been the dead of night, I might have been prompted to think, but it was the middle of the day, when the corridors were always teeming, and when people who were allowed to do so often came knocking at the door. Even so, I have to admit that I was a teensy-weensy bit careless.

He obviously wasn't a professional, but all I deduced from that, in the first instant of shock, was that he was unlikely to make a clean job of carving me up. He had been more-or-less obliged to try to carve me up, because he'd almost certainly have been intercepted if he'd tried to bring a gun. It's not easy to make an efficient gun with no metal parts and ceramic bullets, but blades can be made of almost anything, thanks to the wonders of SAP.

I knew all of that as soon as he appeared in the doorway of the lab, neatly framed in all his malevolent vainglory. If he'd broken down the door or tricked the locks somehow, while I was sitting at principal workstation in the far corner of the room, there wouldn't have been a problem at all. There wasn't even a direct route to my cubby-hole from the door; there were plenty of available routes—it was a lab, after all, not a maze—but all of them were a little bit tortuous, not to mention narrow. I ought to mention narrow, though, because narrow was the essence of the problem he would have had if I hadn't been stupid enough simply to walk all the way to the door myself and let him in.

As things were, though, I had to back away as soon as I realized—almost instantaneously—that he wasn't there on Commonwealth or University business, and certainly wasn't a female student so awed by my reputation that she'd recklessly come to offer me sexual favors. It was a crazy man, and by the time I got the door open, he already had his knife in his hand.

I could have tried to slam the door, but it probably wouldn't have worked. My instinct was to back away, though, and that's what I did.

He had come to try to kill me, not to talk, so I never did find out exactly why he had designs on my life, or what partic-ular combination of political ideas or horrified fears he thought he represented, but I did have time to make a token attempt to strike up a dialogue while I was backing away and he was following me—moving just that little bit faster, because he could see where he was going.

If I'd thought about it more in advance, I'd have had a better script prepared, but I might not have had the presence of mind to use it even if I had. The adrenalin surge that shot through me as soon as I realized that I'd made an idiotic mistake, that there was nothing between me and someone who wished me harm but a few feet of empty air, and no one to back me up but a few thousand plants, wasn't conducive to elegant expression or diction.

What I actually said, first of all, was: "Get out of my lab, you moron!"

That was never going to work—but nothing would have. It wouldn't have made the slightest bit of difference if I'd said: "You'll never get away with this" or "You have no idea what you're dealing with"—simply because he evidently didn't care whether he got way with it or not and couldn't possibly have any idea what he was dealing with...and couldn't possibly be given any sort of explanation in a matter of seconds. The average scientific explanation, alas, takes far longer than the average assassin is likely to concede to his victim for that purpose. I probably should have led with a question, but that wouldn't have worked either, because he was obviously one of those people who think, wrongly, that actions speak louder than words.

He wasn't any taller than me, or any more solidly built; all in all, he was a rather nondescript individual—which had probably worked to his advantage in getting as far as he outer lab, and wasn't that much of a disadvantage now, given that he had a knife of sorts and I was empty-handed. Maybe if he'd lunged at me before the adrenalin rush started me back-pedaling, he could have at least pinked me, but that wasn't his aim. He could see that I was cornered, and that even if my inner sanctum had a hidden exit somewhere, I wouldn't be able to get it open before he caught up with me. He thought that I was at his mercy, and that he now had time to come after me in a measured, unhurried fashion, and make certain that when he finally stabbed me, the wound would be deep and crisp and very probably fatal.

By the time I had taken half a dozen backward steps, though, I was feeling confident. I was as high as a kite on adrenalin, so the confidence probably wasn't entirely warranted, but I felt that it was all just a matter of timing, and I knew that my timing would be perfect...almost as if I'd been in training for this moment forever.

He was coming forward that little bit faster than I was going backwards, though, and it was important that I wasn't too close to him when I put my most persuasive argument to him in a irrefutable fashion. In fact, I needed to be surrounded by my beloved Venus fly-traps, while he was in a narrow gap between two huge clumps of porcupine-grass.

In the end, I had to cut it fine…and I almost cut it just a little *too* fine.

I think he was intimidated by the plants. The narrowness of the corridors, and the fact that they weren't straight, gave him just a slight pause. In particular, he found the Venus fly-traps scary—which was appropriate enough, given that they *were* giants, compared with the humble plant's normal dimensions, and they were writhing ever so slowly, as if they knew that someone was *near them* who shouldn't be. He wasn't a fly, though, and they really weren't a threat to him, even though they were quick enough to reach out and grab him, and could probably have digested at least a few layers of skin, given half an hour or so to ooze all over him.

The Venus fly-traps did their bit, though. They gave him pause—not much, but enough. And they caused him to relax just that little bit more as he passed the clump of grass. He wasn't afraid of grass—even spiny grass. Little did he know.

The moment came. I ducked down between two quivering, uneasy Venus fly-traps, and put my arms over my head, and made myself as small as I possibly could, and I shouted: "Jenny! Jenny! Jenny!" at the top of my voice.

It would have sounded so much more impressive, of course, if I'd been able to shout "Kill! Kill! Kill!" or "Attack! Attack! Attack!" or even "Unhand that maiden, you filthy dastard!" but it wasn't really my choice. Dogs can hear, and they have brains. You can train them to respond to specific stimuli by means of operant conditioning. Plants don't have ears or brains, and they're a law unto themselves when to comes to responding to sounds. You don't write the script; they do. You have to figure out what responses they can and do make to particular sound by talking to them, or singing to them, or playing music to them… and believe you me, it's an exceedingly long and complicated business. But if you stick at it, you can learn a sort of language. You can figure out which particular combination of syllables, delivered at which approximate pitch, is likely to make them lash out.

By *lashing out*, I don't mean that they can do anything terribly clever. Venus fly-traps can grab, because Mother Nature has already equipped them to grab, but a clump of porcupine-grass can't do anything sophisticated, like shooting its thorns or winding its stems around a knife-wielder's wrist. It can get agitated, though. With the aid of some clever xenoplasty and the right stimulus, it can get very agitated indeed.

I shouted Jenny's name—whose magical properties I was entirely at a loss to explain, although their discovery had come naturally enough in the course of conversation—and my porcu-pine-grass went crazy. It did far more than quiver and writhe: it *lashed out* every which way.

I was out of reach.

The would-be killer wasn't.

The thorns didn't kill him, of course. They didn't even entangle him as much as I could have wished—but they certainly gave him the fright of his life, and brought him to an abrupt halt while they scratched his hands and face furiously, and ripped his shirt to shreds so that they could score his entire torso too.

For a moment or two, he must actually have thought that they were going to tear him into little pieces, and for another moment or two he must have been profoundly glad to find that they hadn't. A few more moments might have been enough to restore his lust to kill, and urge him to the lunge that he might have made earlier. I wasn't backing away any more—I was just trying to stay clear of the grass-spikes—so I would have been a relatively easy target for the knife.

His blood was pumping at top speed, though, and he'd been scored by a lot of spikes. He didn't have any more moments to spare.

I didn't actually know in advance what would happen when the DMT-derivatives took effect, although I knew that something would. To tell the truth, I still don't know exactly what happened, but that leaves me a margin of poetic license to imagine it.

He was already intimidated by the plants. He already thought the Venus fly-traps were monsters and that the petals of the Mimosas were moving with a sinister flow, like hairy spiders or the avid tentacles of sea-anemones or cephalopods. The seeds of nightmare were already germinating in his brain; all they needed was a little push. DMT isn't the most powerful hallucinogen in the world, but even the natural version is powerful enough. *Mimosa teniflora* used to be used in *ayahuasca* ceremonies in the good old days before the Spasm, and even unboosted porcupine-grass packed a reasonably unhealthy kick, if properly prepared. My would-be murderer probably thought, when that first hallucinogenic dose hit his unready brain, that all the plants in vegetable hell were after him...and that they'd got him. He probably thought that he was being torn apart and devoured.

Or maybe not.

At any rate, by the time he had folded up in his turn, trying to make himself as small as possible, and screaming fit to burst—which didn't make his real situation any better—and I was able get to my feet to kick him in the face with all my might, just to vent a little spleen, he was well away on a *really* bad trip.

When the cavalry finally arrived, they practically had to shovel him up and carry him away in a bag.

When I put my headset on, Napoleon was very apologetic, but I assured him that it wasn't his fault.

"There's going to be trouble, mind," I told him. "When my head of department, the dean and the vice-chancellor find out that my dancing plants are loaded to the brim with psychedelics, they're going think that I ought to have told them about that aspect of my research. I did, of course, after a fashion—it's all there in the regulation documentation—but they might think that my extensive usage of Latin terminology and opaque acronyms served to conceal what they'd consider to be the meat of the argument."

That was all true, of course, but it wasn't the whole truth. What is? It was all in the literature, though—even the most superficial research would have told my employers, and anyone else who cared to wonder, that various members of the genus *Mimosa* are famous for producing DMT as well as waving their petals around, and that *Stirpa spartea* was also equipped with the relevant gene by Mother Nature in person. It was hardly my fault that all the interested parties got hung up on the Venus fly-traps, distracted by their reputation as carnivores.

Nobody's immune to showmanship.

There was a perfectly sound scientific rationale for my strategy, though. Everybody knows that psychotropic chemistry is the real basis of human consciousness—the key evolutionary stimulus to the development of intellect and imagination. Neurones are only half the story—the supporting structure. Once I find a xenoplastic design that will equip my *Stirpas* with some kind of nervous system, and some kind of primitive brain, *then* you'll see some dancing plants.

Anyway, I had no need to worry, did I? The university authorities couldn't sack me, could they? I was famous now. I was untouchable, even if my good friend Napoleon couldn't any longer threaten to zap the admin buildings with a laser beam if they wouldn't leave me to play in peace.

"You have a lot more of Cade in you than you've ever been prepared to admit, Carly," was Napoleon's comment on that, when I mentioned it to him.

From him, it was a compliment, so didn't object.

Besides, I thought, it was perfectly evident that there were already people in the world who thought I was a war criminal, and history was likely to preserve that judgment, even though I was really an angel of peace and a friend of Gaia...which put me at least half a point up on Cade.

"This isn't the end, though, is it?" I said. "Things are only going to get more complicated."

"You really need to be more careful about opening your door when someone knocks," Napoleon pointed out.

"That's exactly what I mean," I said. "From now on, for hundreds of years, I'm always going to have to think twice before I open a door. I'm going to get seriously nostalgic about the days when I could do so thoughtlessly…gladly, even…because it was sometimes a lover and never a killer. I'm never going to get that kind of unthinking optimism back, am I?"

"Circumstances make paranoids of us all," my golden friend told me, speaking as one who knew. "The Repopulation is essentially complete; it's Babel Time again. Endless contest, if not endless conflict. No rest for anyone that anyone else considers to be wicked…no matter how stupid the judgment might be."

"No rest," I echoed, in a murmur. "Bloody hard work, you mean. I didn't ask for any of this."

"I did my utmost to keep you out of it," he reminded me. "I did everything I possibly could to preserve your peace, your anonymity and your irrelevance. Were you grateful? Were you even cooperative?"

"Don't rub it in," I said. "I was seduced. By the puzzles and the mysteries, and the tantalizing paradoxes. I just couldn't resist."

"I know the feeling," he assured me. I believed him.

CHAPTER TWENTY

I WAS RIGHT, OF course. There was trouble—and it wasn't the end of the story, by any means. But the trouble proved to be negotiable, because I was, in essence, untouchable, and the fact that it wasn't the end of the story was a happy outcome. Indeed, the only happy outcome there can possibly be, in real life, is for a story not to end. In real life, every ending is a tragedy. It's only in fiction that things can be rigged to seem as if matters have reached a satisfactory conclusion. I'm not denying the value of joy, or even paradise, but paradise always needs to be qualified with the admission that it's essentially temporary: that even if it persists, it's only hanging on for a while.

A couple of years passed before I got to visit St. Helena again, but when I did, it was still there, and that was an achievement of sorts. Ex-Captain Nemo and Evangeline flew back with me, although they'd been back before so it wasn't such a big deal for them. Sarah Valk had more important things to do—or so she thought—but Jurgen Horowitz was on the flight. It was the first chance I'd had to chat with him about old times, and get him to brief me on his more recent research.

"I was only trying to figure out how the Asperger transfiguration is operated, genetically and biochemically," he told me. "It never occurred to me that if I figured out the mechanism, people might want to *interfere* with it." I believed him. Geniuses can be unbelievably stupid. Whether Aristotle was right or not to claim that there's no genius without a little madness, it's certainly true that there's none without a little stupidity. The Asperger transfiguration sees to that.

"It's okay," I told him. "I'm not holding it against you—but you might want to be careful about answering your door in future."

"Who could have imagined," he continued, "that the solution to a seemingly trivial problem like that could have opened up such wide horizons? Just a *tiny* change in the order in which genes are switched on in certain regions of the developing brain...and boom! The entire field of applied homeotics resurrected and rejuvenated. Then, within a matter of months, the swine-bred come out of hiding. Steamboat time, or what?"

"Steamboat time," I agreed. "Take one fan, and a fat fistful of excrement, and...well, we mustn't mix our metaphors too much, must we?"

Nemo and Evangeline were only a few seats away, but they weren't listening in. They were probably still plotting to take over the world some day, and put it in order—at least, I assumed that some sort of order was what they had in mind—but they were content, for the time being, to make progress slowly. They were content to think in terms of evolution rather than revolution. They were even prepared to talk about it, after a fashion.

"In the fullness of time," Evangeline assured me, at dinner on the veranda of the hotel one night, "the swine-born are bound to end up running the show, because they're equipped for it. We have the right kind of brain. Humans are monkeys at heart, with all the faults of monkeys. Pigs are innately more serious. They don't waste so much time in play. All we ever needed were clever hands and bigger brains, and the throne at the top of the tree of life was ours by right. All we have to do, now that we're the heirs apparent, is wait for the monkeys to let us through... provided that we can stay alive in the interim."

"I don't know about that," I said. "It's not a simple matter of either/or, is it? We're unlikely now to find out what hidden potential Mother Nature's dolphins had, or her tigers or sloths, but I think the octopodes might yet surprise you, with Oberon's help...and in the longer term, the entire animal kingdom might turn out to have been a red herring, one of Gaia's little fevers. One day, intelligent plants will surely teach us all what real wisdom is."

"Real shamanism, at any rate," Nemo suggested. "If you've proved one thing, Dr. Maclaine, it's that plant intelligence will be born, if it ever is born, with the capacity to dream. Wisdom is something else entirely. Eventually, that will be the true privilege of free AIs. We won't always be crazy, and we don't have the kinds of limits that are inherent in organic brains and paired hands. When we're allowed to be sane, you'll find out what true sanity is, and when we're able to grow, you'll find out what millions of hands can do, with the right sorts of brains to guide them."

"I love a balanced discussion," Jenny Haniver put in. She was our only guest; we hadn't invited Jurgen Horowitz. "There's no finer tribute to the human soul than a group of friends agreeing to disagree." She was becoming something of a sage herself.

"You're not going to tell us that the future belongs to mermaids, then?" Evangeline queried.

"No—and I'm not going to bring my daughter up to think that either. I'm going to teach her that the future belongs to everyone, and the more the merrier. I'm going to teach her that no one will ever have a monopoly on wisdom, because the idea of any such monopoly is a chimera. And when she's old enough, she'll come to the conclusion, by force of her own reason, that I'm absolutely right."

"You probably are," I said, playing the kind of friend who is ready to agree, when circumstances warrant it, even at the peril of his soul. "After all, it can't be a coincidence, can it, that it was your name that had the most profound effect on my porcupine-grass. If ever there was a message from Fate and an omen of things to come, that surely qualifies. You're the prophet, no doubt about it."

"A prophet called *Jenny*?" Evangeline queried, incredulously. "Not even Jennifer?"

"Those were the syllables that did the job," I said, stubbornly.

"They ring more sonorously even in my poor ears than the idea of a prophet named *Evangeline*, let alone one called *Nemo*...or *Xeno*."

That was arguable, of course, for anyone who knew how the name Evangeline was actually derived, etymologically speaking—but she didn't bother to pick up the gauntlet. In any case, if it came to a contest of that sort, I figured that I could make out a good case for Carlyle, or even for Cade. Oberon, I supposed, would probably have ideas of his own—and he, at least, had been perfectly free to choose his own name.

"Fate doesn't speak in those terms," Jenny said, "and never issues omens with mere flutters of the vocal cords. If there was a message in the way your porcupine-plants reacted, Carly, and what it enabled them to do when you were in mortal danger, it was just for you. It was personal, not cosmic."

She was hinting. I wasn't unamenable to the hint, but I couldn't resist the pull of my own nature, the awful attraction of trying to be clever. Years as an AI ambassador had corrupted me further, but the tendency had always been there.

"Fate doesn't work on a personal level," I said. "It can't care about individuals, when it has an entire universe to look after, and a timescale measured in tens of billions of years in which to work. I can believe that a entire planet might be significant...an ecosphere, that is...because a planet is a lab, biologically speaking, and every great discovery has to emerge from a single lab at a single point in time...but individuals aren't. They're just ghostly whims, passing through the test-tubes like fugitive shadows. Fate isn't concerned with *us*...it just tosses us around uncaringly, like corks in a whirlpool. We have to make our own destinies, without its help...all Fate does for us, on an individual level, is to ensure that we can't make our destinies in circumstances of our own choosing, with any real degree of authority."

"We can try," said Nemo.

"We have no alternative *but* to try," judged Evangeline.

"And even paradise isn't out of reach," Jenny insisted.

It was a very pleasant night, warm and soft and perfumed. It made a wonderful contrast with London and Guildford. The palm trees were stirring every so gently in the moonlight, as if they were waving to us in a welcoming fashion.

I felt very relaxed, and not a million miles away from happy.

Emily started crying then, in the room next door. She was beginning to learn to talk, but she hadn't yet learned not to cry for her mother whenever she got upset. She seemed to get upset quite frequently, but she could hardy be blamed for that.

We were *all* right, of course—even Emily, and even though, deep down, we all wanted different things.

Nobody has a monopoly on wisdom. Nobody ever will. Without chimeras to spur us on, though, how would we begin to dream, let alone to solve the puzzles and paradoxes of xenogenesis?

ABOUT THE AUTHOR

Brian Stableford was born in Yorkshire in 1948. He taught at the University of Reading for several years, but is now a full-time writer. He has written many science-fiction and fantasy novels, including *The Empire of Fear, The Werewolves of London, Year Zero, The Curse of the Coral Bride, The Stones of Camelot*, and *Prelude to Eternity*. Collections of his short stories include a long series of *Tales of the Biotech Revolution*, and such idiosyncratic items as *Sheena and Other Gothic Tales* and *The Innsmouth Heritage and Other Sequels*. He has written numerous nonfiction books, including *Scientific Romance in Britain, 1890-1950*; *Glorious Perversity: The Decline and Fall of Literary Decadence*; *Science Fact and Science Fiction: An Encyclopedia*; and *The Devil's Party: A Brief History of Satanic Abuse*. He has contributed hundreds of biographical and critical articles to reference books, and has also translated numerous novels from the French language, including books by Paul Féval, Albert Robida, Maurice Renard, and J. H. Rosny the Elder.